COME SPRING

COME SPRING

Tim LaHaye
and Gregory S. Dinallo

DOUBLEDAY LARGE PRINT HOME LIBRARY EDITION

KENSINGTON BOOKS

KENSINGTON BOOKS are published by

Kensington Publishing Corp.
850 Third Avenue
New York, NY 10022

ISBN 0-7394-5128-6

Printed in the United States of America

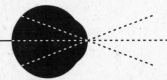

This Large Print Book carries the
Seal of Approval of N.A.V.H.

COME SPRING

Preface

Boston, Massachusetts, February 1918

Europe had been at war for more than three years. British and French forces had fought the Germans to a standstill. More than three million men had already lost their lives. On April 6, 1917, two days before Easter, the United States declared war on Germany; but it would be almost a year before the American doughboys, one million strong, joined the fight.

At the time America was preparing to send her sons to war, the city of Boston had been an intellectually and culturally enriched city of fine universities, art galleries, and salons for almost three hundred years. The cradle of American Independence was also a churning metropolis of tough ethnic neighborhoods and warring political factions. Tickets to the Boston Symphony were as sought after as seats at Fenway Park. Babe Ruth was pitching for the Red Sox. They had won two of the last three World Series. Prohibition would not become law for at least a year. Women would not win the right to vote for more than two years.

Chapter One

A bone-chilling wind swept across the plat-
forms of Boston's North Station as a loco-
motive thundered into view pulling a long
line of coaches. Most of the passengers on
the crowded train were standing at the windows straining to glimpse the city that
would become their new home. Despite the
cold, many of them wore clothing suited to
more temperate climates. One of them, a
young woman, framed by a window that
had been opened, wore a tattered scarf that
fluttered about her face, and cradled a
swaddled infant in her arms as if protecting
it from the crush of people behind her.

Within the tableau of faces were moving
portraits of childlike innocence and worldly
experience, of trembling fear and boundless
hope, of weary acceptance and simmering
rebellion. But it was the face of the young
woman with the infant that had caught

Cooper's eye as the train ground to a stop. Her chin raised in triumph, her eyes aglow with the knowledge that her yearning to be free was about to be realized, her heart thumping in anticipation of a long sought-after new beginning.

Cooper knew what would happen next, and waited patiently with his camera as she made her way to the door with her suitcase and child. As he anticipated, she stepped onto the platform and into the billowing cloud of steam that was coming from the train's wheel housings. Shafts of sunlight, streaming through the vapor that swirled around her, gave the scene a providential glow, intensifying its emotional impact. And in a mere sixtieth of a second, with a decisive click of his shutter, Dylan Cooper had captured this moment for all eternity.

That was weeks ago. And Cooper had taken countless photographs at the train station in the interim; photographs of the poor, the tired and the hungry who—as had Cooper years earlier—survived a harrowing sea voyage, endured the indignities of immigration processing, and made their way to America's towns and cities. Yet the image of the intrepid young woman on the train—

the Madonna and child as Cooper thought of them—had stayed with him; and it was the first negative he developed and printed when he returned to his room on Dorchester Street in South Boston.

The stout Irish woman who ran the rooming house had shown Cooper a large room in the front when he inquired about vacancies. "Two dollars a week. You keep your own house. And you keep to yourself if I make myself clear?"

Cooper nodded as he looked the place over, drawing thoughtfully on his pipe, which was as much a part of him as his camera. "You wouldn't happen to have one with an electric service, now, would you?"

"Indeed, I would. But it's fifty cents more and it's in the back. Electric service," she sniffed, as she padded down the hall, leading Cooper to a room half the size of the first. "I can't imagine what the likes of you would be doin' with that."

The room was disappointingly small but Cooper was pleased to discover that along with its single electric outlet it also had a large closet. And since moving in, he had spent most of his time in the latter, printing photographs with the bare bulb and pull-chain he had rigged on the ceiling, and hunching over the trays of chemicals he used to develop them. He worked round the clock, leaving the closet only when he could no longer stay awake, or—because the strips of leather he had tacked around the door to keep traces of light out, also kept the smell of bromides in—until he could no longer tolerate the choking fumes. And it was here, in this makeshift darkroom, where Dylan Cooper was making the new beginning that had brought him to America.

A confident fellow with a bit of a swagger, Cooper had a mane of unruly salt-and-pepper curls that defied any attempt to control them—much like their owner. He had no doubt he would one day achieve the artistic acclaim that would afford him proper living quarters and more importantly a professionally equipped darkroom with running water and a sink to wash his prints, not to mention a gas-fired heater with a rotating drum to dry them.

For the time being, having spent his last penny on his prized Graflex view camera, he washed them in the tub in the bathroom down the hall—which did little to endear him to those with whom he shared it—and dried them the way local housewives dried their wash: instead of socks, shirts, and underwear, dozens of luminous eight-by-ten-inch prints hung from the clotheslines criss-crossing his room.

Cooper was convinced these were the best pictures he had ever taken. He had no doubt they would be hailed as works of art. He had become obsessed with getting each print just right with a full range of gray tones set off by velvety rich blacks and pure sparkling whites. When the last print had been made, dried, and adjudged perfect, Cooper carefully placed it in a box with others of equal quality; then he took his mackinaw that hung from a nail on the back of the door and left the rooming house, carrying the box under his arm.

A light snow was falling as he hurried to the trolley stop, trailing a stream of pipe smoke behind him. The streetcars that ran along Massachusetts Avenue linked the working-class neighborhoods of Dorchester and Roxbury to the Back Bay area that paralleled the Charles River. Here, the captains of industry lived in limestone mansions close to their offices in the North End where the investment banks and accounting firms that supported their business ventures were located as were the clothiers, antique dealers, and art galleries that catered to their appetite for opulence.

The Van Dusen Gallery, the one that Cooper hoped would exhibit his work, occupied a grand space on the corner of Beacon and Exeter Streets. He walked the few blocks from the trolley stop, his heart pounding from anticipation rather than exertion as he approached the entrance.

Two display easels stood in the window. One held a sign, which in an elegant flowing script proclaimed: *New Impressionist Works*. The other held a large, ornately framed painting entitled: *Poplars on the Banks of the Epte*. It was signed Claude Monet, 1891. A small red tag affixed to the frame indicated it had been sold.

Cooper was about to open the door and step into the vestibule when he noticed a brass plaque next to it that warned: By Appointment Only. The possibility had never occurred to him, and Cooper stood there for a long moment not knowing exactly what to do.

The ornate wrought iron door had a window through which Cooper could see the interior beyond. Raw silk drapery framed the windows. Persian rugs formed an archipelago of subdued color on the parquet floors. Plush sofas allowed clients to commune with a given work prior to acquiring it. A fireplace radiated inviting warmth. Purposely understated to avoid competing with the works of art on display, the sophisticated decor made the brass plaque outside all the more intimidating.

Cooper stepped back and took a deep breath. He had come all the way across town—not to mention across the Atlantic—and was loath to waste the trolley fare. He had come too far to give up so easily, to turn tail and run merely for lack of an appointment. If that was the extent of his gumption, he'd still be in Dumbarton working in the textile mills as his father had before him. He had no doubt the new beginning he sought was on the other side of that door and, after taking a moment to gather his courage, he strode through it purposefully.

Chapter Two

Peter Van Dusen, the gallery's owner, was a highly respected purveyor of fine European painting and sculpture. A natty fellow with a well-groomed beard, he was at his desk in the rear of the gallery tending to paperwork when the bell affixed to the front door rang. It wasn't the gentle tingling that usually announced a client's arrival but a harsh clanging that intensified when the door closed with a jarring slam. Van Dusen flinched at the sound and glared over the top of his spectacles at the man who had charged through the vestibule and was coming straight toward him.

Though the gallery had several rooms, Cooper took no notice whatsoever of the Impressionist masterpieces displayed on their walls, or of the attractive young woman who stood in front of a painting in the splay-footed stance of the dancers it depicted, affixing a red tag to the frame to signify it had been sold.

"Well, it's obvious you're not here to browse," Van Dusen sneered, sweeping his eyes over the wild-haired fellow who stood before him in a threadbare mackinaw dotted with melting snow.

"No, it's not in my nature, sir," Cooper replied, deflecting Van Dusen's salvo. "I've brought you my work. My best work; and if you would—"

"Evidently you failed to notice, or more likely failed to *heed*, my sign," Van Dusen interrupted. "It clearly states: By appointment only. Even my clients do me the courtesy. Don't they, Grace?"

"They certainly do, Mr. Van Dusen," the young woman replied dutifully, stealing a glance at the brash fellow who had dared to arrive unannounced. Tall and willowy with hair the color of amber that was gathered at her neck and swayed behind her, Grace MacVicar looked as if she might have stepped out of a Degas and carried herself in a way that did justice to her name.

Van Dusen slipped a timepiece from his vest and glanced at it. "Speaking of clients, we're expecting one shortly. Show the . . . the *gentleman* out, Grace."

"A client?" Cooper said, paying no attention to the young woman who was trying to guide him toward the entrance. "It wouldn't just happen to be one who's interested in collecting photographs, now, would it?"

"Photographs?" Van Dusen echoed with a derisive cackle. He had assumed Cooper's box contained water colors or pastels, or perhaps a few small scale oils that had become popular. "Photographs? No, sir, I daresay it wouldn't."

"Well, I've a feelin' they might soon as they see mine." Cooper placed the box of prints on the desk and went about opening it.

"I'm not at all amused by your arrogance, sir," Van Dusen said, getting to his feet with an angry huff. He intended to take this crass interloper by the arm and show him the door himself, but the print Cooper had slipped onto the desk caught Van Dusen's eye. He paused mid-stride as if he'd heard a gunshot; then all in one motion, he picked it up and placed it on an easel off to one side of his desk, stepping back to study it. It was the picture of the young mother getting off the train. He did this with another print and another, sighing with emotion at the poetic images: a child's innocent face, eyes filled with hope; a teetering pile of worn suitcases, their contents threatening to burst from within; a farmer's scythe bundled in a flower-patterned bedcover; an elderly man clutching a fishing pole and a crucifix. Van Dusen did this with the growing fervor of a man who, long deprived of his favorite delicacy, had come upon an entire box and couldn't consume them fast enough. "They are extraordinary," he said in an amazed whisper. "Truly extraordinary, Mister . . . ?"

"The name's Cooper," Cooper replied, feeling vindicated as his smile broadened. "*Dylan* Cooper, though Dylan be more than enough."

"Well, Cooper, your work has rare emotional resonance and an astonishing insight into the penumbra of the soul," Van Dusen went on. "The balance of radiant and softened sunlight, the fully envisioned scheme of tonality. They give it a . . . a spirituality that I've never seen in photographs."

"Thank you," Cooper said, genuinely humbled by Van Dusen's praise. "Does that mean you like them well enough to exhibit them?"

Van Dusen turned from the photograph on the easel and settled in his chair, shifting his weight several times as if making a decision. "Yes it does. Believe me, I'm tempted, more than tempted."

"Tempted," Cooper grunted, sensing Van Dusen was burdened. "With all due respect, when I was growing up being tempted meant you were thinking about doin' something you knew you shouldn't be doin'."

Van Dusen broke into a reflective smile. "That is precisely my dilemma."

"If I may?" Grace said in a deferential tone. "I think Mr. Cooper's pictures are all you say and more." Equally captivated, she had moved closer and closer as Van Dusen had placed them on the easel. "In my experience, some temptations are more than worth the risk they require."

"Well, young lady, *my* experience has taught me that this one definitely *isn't*," Van Dusen said, his voice taking on a slight edge. "And neither your personal preference nor mine has anything to do with it." He turned back to Cooper and leaned across the desk as if about to share a confidence. "You see, I'm required to be more disciplined than my outspoken assistant. As much as I like your work, Cooper, I must remind myself that *I* am the seller, not the buyer; and knowing my clients as I do, I don't think they're ready to accept photographs as investment grade art and collect them the way they do paintings and sculpture."

"Maybe they are and maybe they aren't," Cooper protested. "There's really only one way to find out, isn't there?"

Grace nodded in emphatic agreement. "You're outspoken assistant thinks Mr. Cooper makes a valid point, sir. Why not exhibit his work and let your clients decide for themselves?"

The emotion in her voice enriched the lyrical burr of the Highlands Cooper thought he'd detected when she had first spoken, making him smile. "Aye, why not?"

"Because it would be like a shopkeeper stocking his shelves with goods he knows no one is going to buy. I'd be out of business in a month, and"—Van Dusen paused and sent a withering look in Grace's direction—"so would you, I might add." He stepped to the easel, looked longingly at the photograph, then removed it and handed it back to Cooper with the others. "I'm sorry. I hope you understand," he said with a finality that caused Cooper's posture to slacken. "Good luck. You're an extrodinarily talented fellow, Dylan. It was a pleasure seeing your work."

The gallery door creaked open activating the bell, which gave off its gentle tinkle. Van Dusen got to his feet, straightening his waistcoat and hurried toward the vestibule. He greeted his fashionably dressed client effusively and directed her to a room where a number of Cezannes were displayed.

Cooper wasted no time collecting his prints. As soon as he had returned them to the box, he replaced the lid and headed straight for the door, acknowledging Grace with a terse nod as he strode past her.

"Mr. Cooper?" she called out, hurrying after him. Cooper's long strides had taken him to the door by the time she caught up. "Mr. Cooper, I want you to know seeing your work was a pleasure for me, too."

"I daresay you made that quite clear to Mr. Van Dusen," Cooper said, managing an appreciative smile.

Grace responded with one of her own that

could have melted the snow falling outside the window. "It's easy to tell the truth. Besides, we Highlanders have to stick together."

"Aye, I knew I heard it in your voice."

"And I in yours. Dumbarton?"

Cooper nodded.

"As am I. I'm really sorry this didn't work out."

"Not half as sorry as I, believe me," Cooper replied, unable to conceal his bitterness. It was a crushing disappointment and even the sympathies of a lovely young woman couldn't ease the pain of it. "Well, thanks for sticking up for my pictures."

Cooper left the gallery, trudging south in the general direction of Dorchester. The snow had begun to accumulate, and he'd have preferred to take the streetcar, but decided to walk and save the fare. It was a long journey on foot but he had another money-saving reason for making it, not to mention the time it would give him to think about Miss Grace MacVicar from Dumbarton in the Scottish Highlands.

Chapter Three

The weather had turned bitterly cold, and the storms that swept down across New England from Canada had sheathed the city in a shimmering coat of ice.

One morning, about a week before Cooper's visit to the gallery, an elderly resident of the rooming house was found frozen to death in his bed. He'd run out of coal—which working-class Bostonites burned in cast-iron stoves—and didn't have money for more. Cooper, who had already run out of the former, knew the latter would soon be next, and was determined to avoid the poor fellow's fate. Perhaps more importantly, he was also determined to keep the chemicals he used to process his photographs from freezing.

Upon leaving the Van Dusen Gallery, Cooper avoided the main thoroughfares in favor of side streets and back alleys in which he scavenged for anything that would burn. By the time he reached the rooming house, he had a hefty bundle of broken branches, discarded pieces of lumber and the odd fence picket balanced on his shoulder. It was secured at its girth by the leather belt that usually held up his trousers.

Weeks passed. The cold snap prevailed. Soon, Cooper had burned everything he'd gathered as well as the wooden shipping crate that had contained his Graflex, reams of prints that hadn't met his standards, and had since taken to burning newspapers he rolled into logs, along with anything else he could find that would combust. Despite his efforts, he awakened one morning to find his photo processing chemicals frozen in their trays as he had feared. He was beside himself, and on the verge of burning the prints he'd brought to Van Dusen as much for spite as for warmth when someone rapped loudly on his door.

"Mr. Cooper?" the landlady called out in her hoarse brogue. "Mr. Cooper, you in there?"

Cooper was behind in the rent and assumed she was there to collect. He was pleasantly surprised to see Grace MacVicar standing next to her when he opened the door. She was shivering and clutching at the collar of her coat, which seemed unable to keep her warm.

"I explained to 'er we don't fancy gentlemen entertaining ladies in their rooms," the landlady barked. "But she's a pushy one, she is."

"Mr. Cooper is not entertaining me," Grace protested, bristling with indignation. "Nor I him. As I told you, I'm here to discuss a business matter."

"Oh, I'll just bet you are," the landlady cracked with as much sarcasm as she could muster. She stepped forward as Grace entered the room, preventing Cooper from closing the door. "It's no wonder you're in arrears," she hissed with a condemning scowl.

Cooper matched it with one of his own and slowly closed the door, forcing her back into the hallway.

Grace was standing amidst the clotheslines, from which a few prints were still hanging. She was staring with discomfort at the cramped space, her eyes watering at the stinging fumes coming from the makeshift darkroom. Most of Cooper's clothes hung from nails he had driven into the walls. The remainder spilled from an old dresser whose drawers refused to close. A few discarded prints he hadn't yet burned were strewn on the floor. Grace stepped to the cast-iron stove to warm her hands but it was cold. "Oh, dear," she said, clearly troubled by Cooper's living conditions. "Now I know what they mean by starving artists."

"It's *freezing* artists this time of year," Cooper joked, concealing his embarrassment and getting a smile out of her. "Now what kind of business might you be here to discuss, Miss MacVicar?"

"Mr. Van Dusen's business," Grace replied, barely able to contain herself. She opened her purse and presented Cooper with an envelope on which *Dylan Cooper, Photographer* had been written in elegant script.

Cooper tore it open and found an equally well-scripted note on Van Dusen's stationery, which asked if he would come to the gallery at his earliest convenience and bring along his prints. It was signed: *With utmost sincerity and admiration, Peter Van Dusen.*

Cooper's heart was pounding in his chest.

"Does this mean what I think it means?" he asked, afraid to commit to it.

"It certainly does, Mr. Cooper."

"He's decided to exhibit my pictures?"

Grace responded with an emphatic nod.

"I can't imagine why?" Cooper prompted with a suspicous smile that suggested she was responsible.

"Oh, no, Mr. Cooper. I had nothing to do with it, if that's what your thinking."

"Well, Mr. Van Dusen's not the type to change his mind on a whim. There's got to be a reason for it."

"Of course there is," Grace said. "Dozens of them." She recognized the box that Cooper had brought to the gallery atop a dresser and fetched it, deftly making her way between the clotheslines en route. "They're in this box."

"Oh, I've no doubt he's taken with my work," Cooper said, charmed by her unflagging spirit. "What I can't fathom is why it's investment grade art now when just weeks ago it wasn't. The man's a businessman first and foremost. I can't imagine it doesn't have something to do with *business*." He spat out the last word, emphasizing his distaste for it.

"Well, I'm afraid you'll have to ask Mr. Van Dusen about that," Grace said, supressing a smile that would have made Cooper suspect she knew more than she was telling if he'd seen it. "Shall we go?"

Cooper didn't want to appear eager and briefly considered having her tell Van Dusen he'd come by in a few days, but his circumstances made such posturing impractical. He slipped into his mackinaw, took the box of photographs from Grace, and led the way to the trolley stop.

Like all the streetcars that crisscrossed the heart of Boston, the Massachusetts Avenue trolley locked onto a steel cable that ran beneath the street to move forward, and released it to stop. Consequently, it lurched toward its destination in an unnerving series of fits and starts, its bell clanging loudly at every stop, which seemed to be at just about every corner. By the time it reached the Back Bay, Cooper and Grace had spent more than an hour being jostled in the unheated car. They went straight to the fireplace when they reached the gallery. Its walls were bare. Since Cooper's last visit, the Impressionist masterpieces had been crated and shipped to the wealthy collectors who had purchased them.

Van Dusen took custody of Cooper's box and began laying the prints out across a table that ran beneath the window. "Astonishing . . ." he gushed, pausing at each one before setting it down. "Simply astonishing . . . even better than I remembered." He whirled to his desk, the tails of his coat flying about as he settled in his chair, and began turning the pages of his calendar. "Opening night is . . ."

"Two weeks Monday," Grace said before he found it.

Cooper's head snapped around from the fireplace in reaction. "The opening's in two weeks?"

"Not much time to install a show, is it?" Van Dusen prompted anxiously.

"I think Mr. Cooper and I can manage."

"Speak for yourself, lass," Cooper said. "It could take longer than that just to lay out the show properly, not to mention—" He paused suddenly at something that dawned on him. "Two weeks . . ." he repeated to himself, thinking aloud.

Grace nodded.

So did Cooper, in a way that suggested

he had just figured something out. *Now we're getting to work on the crust of the bread,* he thought. As he'd told Grace at the rooming house, he sensed that there was more to Van Dusen's change of heart than an appreciation of his photographs, sensed that there had to be some business angle to it, and now he sensed just what that angle was. "Correct me if I'm wrong, Mr. Van Dusen, but I've been around long enough to know that galleries book their exhibitions months if not years in advance, don't they?"

"You're wrong," Van Dusen fired back. "Each gallery has its scheduling habits. Of course there is always the odd situation that—"

"*Very* odd in this case," Cooper interrupted, now convinced by Van Dusen's hair-trigger reaction. "Something's going on here, Mr. Van Dusen, and if you and I are going to do business, you'll need to put your cards on the table first."

"I thought what was going on here was plainly obvious," Van Dusen said, shifting in his chair. "After some reflection, I decided you were right. There *is* only one way to test the market for photographs as fine art, and your work has the best chance I've seen of success. Those are my cards, Mr. Cooper, and they've been on the table ever since you came barging into my gallery . . . without an appointment, I might add."

"Aye, but they're still not all face up, yet, are they?" Cooper went on, raising the ante. "You see, when you turn them *all* over, when they're *all* staring you square in the eye, it starts lookin' more and more like I'm the one who's doing you the favor not the other way round. That's the truth of it. Isn't it?"

Van Dusen squirmed in discomfort. His eyes darted to Grace with an accusing stare. "I thought I made it clear you weren't to mention our . . . situation."

Grace held his look and nodded smartly. "*Very* clear, sir. And I didn't."

"You're certain."

"Whatever your . . . *situation*," Cooper said, about to lose his temper, "she didn't breathe a word of it to me, despite my prompting. Now out with it."

Van Dusen glared at him over his spectacles, then his expression softened, and he nodded in concession. "All right Cooper, you've more than earned the truth. I hope you can accept it."

"There's only one way to find out, isn't there?" Cooper said pointedly.

"The truth is—" Van Dusen paused. He got to his feet and came around the desk to be face to face with Cooper. "The truth is, one of the artists I represent is a temperamental fellow who, quite unfortunately and unnecessarily, doubts his talent. So much so, that at the last minute he decided his current work wasn't up to his standards and insisted I reschedule his show."

"In other words, you'd much prefer to be opening an exhibiton of his work in two weeks than mine."

"You asked for the truth," Van Dusen said, coolly.

Cooper's jaw tightened, his eyes hardened to angry pinpoints. "As a matter of fact, if it wasn't for him, for this temperamental fellow, you wouldn't be giving me this show at all, would you? *That's* the truth. Isn't it?!"

Grace knew what the answer would be and winced in anticipation of Cooper's reaction.

Van Dusen nodded with apprehension. "I'm afraid so. You see, Cooper, the only thing worse than a gallery full of artwork that might not sell, is a gallery without any artwork to sell at all."

Cooper was stung by the sheer crassness of Van Dusen's reply. He stood there for a long moment, absorbing the impact, then looked over at Grace. Her eyes were glistening with emotion, her face an alluring image of empathy and concern. Despite the unnerving circumstances, he couldn't help thinking it was an image he'd have given anything to capture with his camera. Instead, it was Cooper who'd been captured, taken prisoner by her eyes, which were pleading with him to accept the truth—the truth he'd demanded. It wasn't long before the fight went out of him. He broke into a smile. "Then I guess this is my lucky day, isn't it?"

"I wasn't sure you'd see it that way," Van Dusen said with a relieved sigh. "But I'm quite pleased you did. Now while we're at it, you wouldn't happen to have any other questions, would you, Mr. Cooper?"

"Aye, as a matter of fact I do . . ."

Van Dusen rolled his eyes and looked over at Grace who was now laughing to herself, clearly taken by Cooper's incorrigible behavior.

"Why is the opening to be on a work day?" Cooper asked, clearly puzzled by it. "Why not a weekend when people have time to . . . to browse, so to speak?"

"Perhaps, the people *you* know," Van Dusen replied, filling with self importance. "But the people *I* know . . . well, they're all either skiing in Vermont or sailing off the Cape on the weekend."

"He's right, Mr. Cooper," Grace said, stepping in to make sure they didn't go at it again. "Openings are always on Monday night. The theaters are dark, the week's social whirl has yet to start, and the buyers, not to mention the critics and reviewers are all back in town with nothing to do."

"Exactly," Van Dusen said. "Simply put, if you had a choice between spending the evening in a gallery looking at photographs, or at the theater with a vivacious young woman on your arm, which would it be?"

"I'd be looking at photographs," Cooper replied, deadpan; then glancing over at Grace, he quickly added, "With a *lovely* young woman on my arm."

Van Dusen chuckled heartily. "You won't be the first to ask or the first to be turned down."

Cooper questioned Grace with a puzzled look.

"I usually don't attend openings, Mr. Cooper," she explained, demurely. "I prefer to spend my evenings at home, but I just might make an exception in your case."

"I've a good feelin' about this," Cooper said, heartened by her response and all that had happened.

"So do I," Grace said, scooping a fistful of red sold tags from Van Dusen's desk. "Photography's time has come. This show is going to sell out."

"Well, I'm *tempted* to agree," Van Dusen chimed in with a mischievous twinkle at his choice of words. "The difference is . . . I've learned from bitter experience not to trust it."

Chapter Four

"We've a lot of work to do and little time to do it," Van Dusen said when the excitement had worn off and the full impact of their deadline hit home. He cocked his head in thought, then glanced to Cooper. "We'll need a second set of prints to lay out the show. I assume you have test prints, discards that weren't sharp enough, or lacked the proper tonal range . . ."

"Aye, more than I care to admit," Cooper replied, lighting his pipe as he continued. "Sometimes it takes ten just to get one that's right. I've been burning 'em for warmth, but I always keep one of each as a record."

"Good," Van Dusen said, gesturing to the prints he had placed on the table. "Because these, the originals so to speak, will be at the framers with you."

Cooper looked puzzled. "With me? At the

framers? And what am I going to be doing there?"

"What you and only you can do, Mr. Cooper . . ." Van Dusen replied, with an enigmatic pause. ". . . making certain that each and every one of these magnificent photographs is properly framed."

"Nonsense," Cooper scoffed. "It's the picture that matters, not the frame; and since they're all eight-by-tens, couldn't we just order enough mattes and frames of a certain size and style and be done with it?"

"We could. But it would be a mistake. A very *costly* one," Van Dusen replied in crisp bursts that rang with authority. "We're presenting photographs as fine art, Cooper—as *investment grade* art—which mandates we emphasize their uniqueness. If I'm going to advise my clients to collect them as they would paintings, each print must be framed as if it were a painting. The tone and texture of the matte, the amount of breathing space between image and frame, not to mention the style and finish of the frame itself must all be selected with an eye to the subject matter and mood of a given picture. *And*—I hasten to add—it's not open for discussion."

"No need for any," Cooper said, raising a brow in tribute as he exhaled a stream of pipe smoke. He was impressed by Van Dusen's shrewd analysis of the market, and pleased at his commitment to photography as fine art. He wasn't pleased to learn that the framer's workshop was in Quincy about an hour's train ride from his rooming house in the opposite direction from where the gallery was located.

While Cooper spent his days in Quincy working with the framers, Grace spent them in the gallery working with the set of discarded prints he had provided. With Van Dusen's guidance, she tacked them up and moved them about from wall to wall, grouping them by subject and mood, in compliment and contrast. Each was hung and re-hung until she and Van Dusen were satisfied that each picture on its own, as well as in relation to the others, made a striking and compelling presentation.

When he wasn't consulting with Grace, Van Dusen focused on getting out invitations to clients, critics and reviewers, and placing advertisements in newspapers and society journals. Both heralded an exhibition of works by a new talent he had discovered—an exhibition which he had titled: *In Search of New Beginnings. The Photographs of Dylan Cooper.*

Almost two weeks had passed by the time Cooper finished his work with the framers; weeks during which he hadn't seen Grace. He arrived at the gallery as anxious to see her as he was to see his pictures displayed on its walls.

She looked even more beautiful than he remembered. Her hair pulled back from her face that glowed with the vitality and strength of character that so attracted him. "You've done a fine job, lass," he said on seeing the groupings she'd made. Then he cocked his head with uncertainty and pulled the tacks from the corners of a print that had caught his eye, exchanging it with another. "Though I might be able to improve on it a little here and there."

"Might you, Mr. Cooper?" Grace said, pretending she was shocked. "I never thought a gentleman of your reserve could be so opinionated."

"Nor I," Van Dusen said, unable to keep a straight face as Cooper and Grace erupted with laughter.

The next morning, when the framed prints

were delivered, the three of them went about replacing each of the discards that had been used to lay out the show with its beautifully framed mate. And soon, the walls that had, just weeks before, displayed Renoirs, Degas, Monets, and Cezannes, now displayed—as the placard in the gallery's window proclaimed—The Photographs of Dylan Cooper.

As soon as they had finished hanging the framed prints, Van Dusen collected the set of discards and threw them into the fireplace.

"Wait," Cooper protested. "There's no need to be destroying those."

"Of course there is," Van Dusen replied, as the flames consumed them. "This may be an exhibition of photographs, but as of tonight, they're all one of a kind works of art; and I don't want any copies about." He paused, with that mischievous twinkle Cooper had seen before and added, "Of course, you can always print more if need be."

"Aye," Cooper said, unmollified. "I was planning on using those to heat my room."

Van Dusen emitted an amused cackle. "Have faith, Cooper. If all goes well tonight, you'll never have to worry about that again. Go home, have a bath, and be back here by five-thirty in your Sunday best."

Before walking to the trolley stop, Cooper stood outside the gallery staring at the placard that displayed his name, and at the sparkling photograph on the easel next to it—the picture of the young mother getting off the train. Now officially titled, Madonna and Child, the print had been matted with pale gray linen and set in a frame that had a burnished silver finish that gave it a befitting Renaissance grandeur.

It is only a matter of time now, Cooper thought. Perhaps days, a few weeks at most before his talent would be recognized and he'd be hailed as the fine artist he was, his works included in important private collections and displayed in major museums.

Grace had noticed him slip out the door and had been watching him from the vestibule. "You still can't believe it, can you, Mr Cooper?" she prompted as she came outside to join him.

"Aye, a dream come true," Cooper said, drawing thoughtfully on his pipe.

"I'd give you a penny for them if I had one to spare," Grace prompted.

"I wouldn't take it if you had," Cooper said with an amused chuckle. "It's not fair for the person in your thoughts to be paying for them."

"I see," Grace mused curiously. "And just what were you thinking about the person in your thoughts?"

"Oh, just that perhaps it's time she considered calling me by my Christian name."

"Fine, Mr. Cooper, I'll see to it she does just that."

Cooper laughed good-naturedly. "Why am I gettin' the feeling I'll be a dodderin' old man before I hear the name, Dylan, come from your lips?"

"I've no idea. As a matter of fact the next opportunity I have to call you, Dylan, Dylan, I'll be sure and do so."

A smile that left no doubt of his fondness for her broke across Cooper's face. "You've got a lovely way about you, Grace."

"Most people from Dumbarton do," she said, leaving no doubt she was returning the compliment.

"Then, in the spirit of us Highlanders sticking together, shall I take that to mean you'll consider coming to the opening tonight?"

"You mean even though I prefer to spend my evenings at home?"

Cooper nodded with resignation. "Aye, even though . . ."

"Okay, I shall. That's a promise."

"I'm afraid I'm not sure what it is you're promising, Grace. To consider it? Or to be there?"

Grace looked up at him, waiting until his eyes had found hers; then in a wistful tone that intensified the moment, she said, "I'll be there, Dylan. I promise."

Chapter Five

The night of the opening turned out to be the first in weeks that the temperature had crept above freezing. The sky had the clarity of crystal and an umbrella of stars shone upon the city of Boston.

Likewise, the Van Dusen Gallery glowed like a jewel in the darkness. Shafts of light from its windows spilled across the cobblestones as a line of horseless carriages queued on Exeter Street. There was nary a Model-T in sight as one handcrafted motorcoach after another pulled up to the gallery, depositing their well-dressed and well-heeled passengers at its entrance. As Van Dusen had hoped, the more clement weather had prompted the upper crust of Boston's social register to turn out en masse. Those who had money. Those who had lineage. Those who had power. And those who had all three.

As the guests entered the vestibule, valets

in formal attire helped them from their great-coats and floor-sweeping furs, then directed them inside where uniformed waiters, balancing trays, slithered deftly through the crowded rooms dispensing flutes of champagne, along with canapes and hors d'oeuvres.

Van Dusen worked each room like a patriarch at a family reunion. He lived for opening nights, for those moments when he presented an artist's works to those whom he knew would not only appreciate them, but could also afford to *continue* appreciating them on the walls of their homes, offices, and clubs. As he circulated among his esteemed clientele, they toasted him and the new talent he had discovered with congratulations and praise that went beyond the superlative.

Van Dusen basked in the accolades, but was more interested in the snippets of conversation he overheard in passing, in what the animated cliques of clients, critics, and reviewers were saying to each other when they didn't know he was listening. And soon, having heard phrases that extolled Cooper's "unique artistic expression," his "images of emotional intensity," and his "stunning insight into the human condition," emanating from every room in the gallery,

Van Dusen knew that their enthusiasm for Cooper's work was indeed genuine.

Cooper heard the accolades as well and was visibly delighted, but he'd have preferred a tumbler of Laphroaig or a tankard of Guiness to the flute of Veuve Clique he held between thumb and forefinger. Try as he might, he mingled awkwardly at best, feeling out of place in his corduroys, plaid shirt, and tweed sports coat. Despite his discomfort, the collectors and haughty society matrons found Cooper's bohemian style charming and passed him on from one group to another, showing him off as if he were a newly acquired bauble, which made him feel all the more uncomfortable.

"I'm curious about the wellspring of your creative energy and insight, Mr. Cooper," one of the women who'd been fawning over him asked.

"Have you a muse?" another chimed in, eyeing him as she had the caviar she'd been devouring. "Or are you in search of one?"

"Aye, I'm always in search of amusement," Cooper replied, eliciting a chorus of laughter.

"Please tell us all about the source of your inspiration," a third prompted. "Is it external? Or does it all come from somewhere deep inside you?"

"I'm afraid all that ever comes from deep inside me are clouds of pipe smoke and the occasional belch."

The group of women thought it was hilarious and erupted with more laughter. Cooper used the distraction to disengage. The one person he wanted to see at the opening wasn't there. Every chance he got, he scanned the crowded rooms of the gallery in search of her, his eyes darting anxiously to the door in the vestibule with each tinkle of its bell.

Suddenly, he glimpsed her standing amid a group of people who were off in a corner, and began working his way toward them. He was reaching out to touch her arm when she sensed his presence and turned, revealing that she wasn't Grace MacVicar at all but a woman of similar height and hair color who swept her eyes over his attire and said, "Something tells me you're Mr. Cooper, aren't you?"

"Aye, guilty as charged, ma'am," Cooper replied.

"Well, Mr. Cooper, where *do* you get such artistic inspiration and insight?"

"I'm afraid it comes from somewhere deep inside me, ma'am," Cooper replied, trying not to roll his eyes, which had finally, beyond doubt, located the one person they had spent the evening searching for.

Radiant in a black dress of the simplest fashion Grace seemed to float just above the floor as she moved across it with a group of gentlemen who encircled her.

Cooper fought to keep her in sight, catching a glimpse of her here, a glimpse there among the crisscrossing waiters and swirling crowd that suddenly closed in around her, blocking his view. He quickened his pace, weaving between the knots of people that separated them when several of the group around Grace stepped aside to pursue a waiter with a tray of champagne flutes, revealing the Scottish goddess in their midst.

Cooper's heart, which had been fluttering like a schoolboy's, sank like the *Lusitania* at the sight of her—at the sight of Grace MacVicar on the arm of a handsome, well-dressed fellow in his early thirties. Tall with the strapping build of an athlete, he was guiding Grace through the crowd in Cooper's direction with a degree of ease and familiarity that suggested they were more than casual acquaintances.

Chapter Six

Cooper was crestfallen. He needed all the time it took for Grace and her escort to reach him to marshall his courage and stand his ground to greet her. "Miss MacVicar," he said, forcing a smile. "I'm so pleased you could come."

"As am I, Mr. Cooper," Grace replied. She spoke in a formal tone and averted her eyes, which wasn't at all like her. "I'd like to introduce you to someone," she said, turning to the young man who had her arm. "Mr. Cooper, may I present . . ."

Before Grace could finish, the young fellow took hold of Cooper's hand and, shaking it vigorously, said, "Colin . . . Colin MacVicar. A pleasure to meet you, sir."

MacVicar? Colin MacVicar?! *How could I have been such a fool?!* Cooper thought, as it dawned on him that Colin was neither a suitor, nor her betrothed as he had feared on first seeing them together, but her husband!

His mind was racing fast as if, having fallen from a cliff, his entire life was passing before him in a matter of seconds; and he wasted no time chastising himself for coveting a young woman who was married. In truth he wanted nothing more than to crawl into a peat bog and never be seen again. For the life of him, he couldn't fathom how he could have failed to sense it! Or how she could have failed to mention it! Of course, when he added up the hours they'd spent in each other's company, he quickly realized it had hardly been the better part of a day. Other than each knowing the other was from Dumbarton, they hardly knew anything about each other at all. But hadn't Van Dusen referred to her as *Miss* MacVicar? Wasn't her ring finger bare of adornment, marital or otherwise? In the blink of an eye, his mind had raced through every permutation and possibility, and was racing on to the next when Grace, who had seen the panic in his eyes, said, "Colin is my brother, Mr. Cooper. I don't believe I've had the opportunity to mention him."

Cooper concealed his relief, managing

not to blurt out, Thanks be to God! which were the words that came immediately to mind. "The pleasure's all mine," he said with a thin smile. "Believe me."

"On the contrary, sir, it's mine," Colin said with evident sincerity. "I'm quite enjoying your work. Especially those that suggest biblical themes."

"Aye, some of the greatest stories ever told in the Bible: famine, pestilence, destruction, death . . . The scripture is filled with themes that bring powerful images to mind."

Colin nodded and forced a smile. "I was thinking less of the Apocalypse and more of those like the one in the window. I believe it's titled Madonna and Child, isn't it?"

Cooper nodded emphatically. "Aye, it's a fine picture." He was desperately in search of a way to jettison Colin and have Grace to himself for a few moments when he spotted Van Dusen nearby, and sensed he had found it. "Mr. Van Dusen?" Cooper called out. "Mr. Van Dusen, this gentleman has expressed a strong interest in the Madonna."

"Oh, an excellent choice, sir," Van Dusen said, warming up his sales pitch as Cooper knew he would. "I may be wrong but I'm fairly certain it isn't yet spoken for. Why don't we step aside where we can discuss its acquisition?" Before Colin could protest or explain, Van Dusen was leading the way toward his desk in the rear of the gallery.

"Your brother!" Cooper hissed in an incredulous whisper as he took Grace aside. "I've a feeling *he's* the one who prefers you spend your evenings at home."

"He's my *eldest* brother, Dylan," Grace explained. "He worries about me. It's a long story."

"I'm all ears, lass."

"This is neither the time, nor the place. Suffice it to say, when I mentioned I was coming tonight, he insisted on coming along as my chaperone."

Cooper grunted and cocked his head in the direction of a group of young men who were preening nearby. "From the looks of these art lovers, you'll probably need one before the night's over."

"I can take care of myself, I assure you," Grace said, starting to laugh.

"Oh, I've no doubt of it, lass, it seems it's Doubting Colin who does."

"Shush," Grace said, putting a finger to her lips, which helped keep her from laughing even harder. She noticed Colin had extricated himself from Van Dusen and was making his way through the crowd in their direction. "He's coming this way."

"Ah, there you are," Colin said as he approached.

"How did you and Mr. Van Dusen get on?" Cooper prompted with as casual an air as he could muster.

"Uncomfortably at best," Colin replied. "Somehow he mistook my *interest* in your work for a wish to acquire it. I'm afraid we should be going, Grace."

"Oh, Colin, no. Not yet. It's much too early."

"Yes, I know, but I'm afraid we really must."

"If you don't mind me asking, Colin, just what is it that you're so afraid of?" Cooper teased, an edge creeping into his voice.

"Of missing the streetcar, Mr. Cooper," Colin replied, matching his tone. "Our line stops running in less than an hour."

"Then we'll leave in *half* an hour," Grace said with finality. "I'm sure we'll have little trouble managing the stop in time." It was clear she intended to spend every one of those thirty minutes with Cooper. As she proceeded to move about the gallery on his arm, he seemed to overcome his awkwardness and enjoy the ongoing attention and accolades with a degree of comfort that had eluded him prior to her arrival.

The next morning, Grace was up at the crack of dawn, and left the apartment in East Cambridge she shared with her brother earlier than usual. She used the extra time to buy copies of all the newspapers at the stand opposite the trolley stop. Once on the streetcar, she tore through their pages searching for the reviews of Cooper's show, and read them all during the ride to the gallery.

Several janitors were dealing with the evening's aftermath—collecting the empty champagne flutes, half-eaten hors d'oeuvres, discarded napkins, and engraved invitations the guests had left strewn about— when Grace arrived. She found Cooper and Van Dusen slouched in chairs on opposite sides of Van Dusen's desk, drinking cups of black coffee. Both men were wearing the clothing they had worn the previous evening and appeared disheveled and subdued. It seemed to Grace as if they had spent the night there, which they had; though the amber-stained tumblers and empty bottle of malt whiskey on the desk suggested it wasn't coffee they had been drinking. *Boys will be boys,* she thought, realizing their current state was the result of their celebrating well into the wee hours of the morning.

The thwack of the newspapers Grace dropped on the desk pulled them from their stupor. "The reviews are all we'd hoped for and more," she said, bristling with excitement. "'Cooper's work soars to new artistic heights,'" she went on reading aloud from them. "'An eye for the human condition as sharp as an eagle in search of prey . . . Images of astonishing power that one won't soon forget.' And, believe it or not, someone from *Camera Work* was there!"

"Camera Work?" Cooper echoed, his head snapping around at the mention of the New York based, Alfred Steigliz-edited quarterly—the country's leading journal of avant-garde art and criticism. "How, pray tell, do you know that?"

Grace held up one of the reviews. "Because it says so right here," she replied, giving full rein to her enthusiasm. "It seems the art critic from the *Globe* is their Boston correspondent. It says *Camera Work* is planning to reprint his review and do a profile of 'the ever so talented photographer Mr. Dylan Cooper' . . . which means New York collectors will soon be making a pilgrimage to Boston—if there are any photographs left for them to collect!" She scooped a bundle of red sold tags from Van Dusen's desk and held them aloft in triumph, then began sorting through the papers on it in search of something.

"You're wasting your time, Grace," Van Dusen said, knowing what she was looking for. "It's not there."

"Well, would you mind telling me how I'm going to tag the ones that are spoken for without a sales list?"

"There is no sales list, Grace," Van Dusen replied.

"Does that mean you've misplaced it? Or that you've decided to keep which ones are spoken for and by whom in your head?"

Van Dusen stroked his beard, then glanced to Cooper and prompted him with a nod.

"I'm afraid none of my pictures are spoken for, Grace," Cooper explained, lowering his eyes as if shamed by it. "Not even one."

Grace stiffened, her head cocked at an angle that reflected her incredulity. The previous evening, she and Colin had been among the earliest to leave the gallery, hurrying off just as the opening was hitting its stride; and having heard nothing but praise for Cooper's work, and having just finished reading the reviews, she had every reason to believe it had been a resounding success. "Not even one . . ." she repeated, realizing that they'd been up the entire night commiserating, not celebrating, as she had thought.

"I'm afraid not, Grace," Van Dusen said with a look that left no doubt of it.

"Oh, dear," Grace sighed, her eyes glistening with emotion at the knowledge that Cooper was undoubtedly heartbroken. "But things are bound to change when they see these, aren't they?" she prompted, brandishing some of the reviews. "And then there's *Camera Work*, too!"

Van Dusen shook his head no. "I don't think they'll make one iota of difference, Grace."

"Why not? Why are you being so pessimistic?"

"Because all the major collectors have already made their decision; and no matter how complimentary those reviews, and any to come, may be, they haven't a chance of changing it."

"But everyone who was here last night loved Dylan's pictures, each and every one of them," she protested with characteristic tenacity.

"Indeed they did," Van Dusen replied. "As a matter of fact, I'd go so far as to say many were even *tempted* to buy them . . . and I've no doubt they would have, had they been paintings. The problem isn't with Dylan's pictures, Grace, it's with photography."

Cooper nodded with resignation. "I said there was only one way to find out if collectors would accept photographs as fine art. Well, the answer is no. Mr. Van Dusen was right from the start."

And Van Dusen *was* right. Weeks passed. The pictures hung unspoken for on the gallery walls. And with each passing day, it became clear that, though Cooper was roundly toasted as an exceptional talent, the accolades hadn't turned into sales and never would. As Van Dusen had initially feared, collectors weren't ready to accept photographs as investment grade art.

Chapter Seven

"It's been weeks, Dylan. Where have you been?" Grace's voice rang with a mixture of anger and relief as Cooper entered the gallery and strode toward her in his lumbering gait. "I came by your room. I left messages with your landlady . . ."

"Aye," Cooper said, his eyes sweeping across the gallery's walls. Grace and Van Dusen were in the process of taking down his photographs, and many of them were bare. "The one about the show closing was waiting for me when I got back this morning. So, I thought I'd better come by and collect my work."

"Back from where?" Grace wondered.

"Nowhere," Cooper grunted sullenly. "Camping."

"In this cold?" she said, chastising him like a misbehaving child.

Cooper responded with a disheartened

shrug and took a moment to light his pipe. "I was in need of some solitude and soul-searching."

Grace sighed, her eyes softening with empathy. "You mustn't lose faith in yourself, Dylan. You mustn't make the mistake of doubting your talent. *I* certainly haven't."

"Nor have I," Van Dusen added. "I've no doubt they'll all be collector's items one day."

Cooper exhaled a stream of pipe smoke and smiled thinly. "You're just saying all this to lift my spirits from the gutter, aren't you?"

"Go to church if you want your spirits lifted," Van Dusen retorted. "I meant what I said about your pictures, and I'm prepared to prove it."

"Prove it, eh?" Cooper challenged. "And how do you propose to do that? By buying them all yourself?"

"No, by storing them here until my clients do, and providing you with a stipend in the meantime."

Cooper recoiled as if offended. "A stipend? Am I to understand you're offering me money?"

Van Dusen nodded smartly. "It won't keep you in champagne and caviar; but frugal fellow that you are, I've no doubt it will keep you afloat."

Cooper's face reddened with embarrassment. The idea of finding himself the subject of such an offer, let alone in front of Grace, was a devastating blow to his pride. "I prefer to sink or swim on my own, Mr. Van Dusen. Truth be told, I've no need of assistance; and if the state of my finances was dire, which I assure you it isn't, I still couldn't be taking your money."

"You wouldn't be *taking* it, Cooper," Van Dusen explained, about to lose his patience. "It would be a loan against future sales. I've done it with promising artists before, and I've never been sorry."

Cooper's eyes widened in reaction.

"That's right," Van Dusen said, seeing it. "You're not the first artist in Boston to find himself behind in his rent."

"Where, pray tell, did you get that idea?"

Van Dusen squirmed in discomfort and exchanged an apprehensive glance with Grace.

"From me," she said in a forthright tone. "Your landlady kept asking me if I knew where you were. When I asked why she wanted to know . . ." Grace let it trail off, suggesting the rest was obvious. "There's no shame in accepting help, Dylan. It won't leave some indelible stain on your soul, you know."

"I'm afraid it's already been blackened beyond redemption, lass," Cooper joked, trying to save face. "It's generous of you, Mr. Van Dusen, but as I said I've always managed on my own, and I've no intention of changin' now. None whatsoever."

"I don't know why you're being so stubborn, but suit yourself," Van Dusen conceded. He was concerned Cooper wasn't up to taking advice, but decided to speak his mind regardless. "Don't take this the wrong way, but under the circumstances, you might be wise to consider commercial photography for a while."

"Commercial work?" Cooper bristled, perceiving it as an insult as Van Dusen had feared.

"I'm your friend, not your enemy, Cooper," Van Dusen counseled evenly. "It won't cost anything to hear me out."

Cooper responded with an indulgent nod.

"I was chatting with one of my clients," Van Dusen went on. "His name's Latour, Georges Latour. You might recall him from the opening? A rather flamboyant chap. French accent. Somewhat full of himself."

"They were all full of something, I recall that," Cooper cracked. "But if I had the pleasure of meeting Mr. Latour, I'm afraid it escapes me."

"Well, he was there, and as it happens he's a—"

"Aye, for all the good it did me."

"If you'll do me the courtesy of listening, he might do you some good *now*," Van Dusen snapped in a tone that silenced Cooper. "As I was saying, he's a merchant, an extremely successful one. His emporium on Marlborough Street sells expensive and fashionable European haut couture for women."

"Quite fashionable, indeed," Grace said, her eyes brightening at the mention of it. "Georges Latour . . . Every woman in Boston wishes she could shop there."

"It just so happens," Van Dusen went on, "that he's looking for someone to photograph his Spring collection. The pictures will be used in newspaper advertisements, which he's planning to—"

Cooper nearly bit through his pipe stem. "Fashion photography?" he erupted, stung

by an insult which, as far as he was concerned, exceeded that of the stipend.

"The job would pay well," Van Dusen
pressed on, ignoring the outburst. "And
since he was quite taken with your work, I'm
certain he would—"

"I'm certain of it too!" Cooper roared. "But
there's not enough money on God's good
earth to tempt Dylan Cooper to take on an
assignment in . . . in . . ." He paused and, as
if spitting out something distasteful, growled,
"Advertising!"

"Well, the decision's yours, Cooper," Van
Dusen said, managing to keep his composure. "Think it over and let me know."

"Oh, I need no such assurance," Cooper
said, his eyes hardening to angry pinpoints.
"When it comes to my pictures, the decision
has always been mine! And always will be
mine!"

"There's no need to get upset. It was just
a figure of speech and I—"

"Furthermore," Cooper went on, "there's
no need to think it over because the decision's already been made. I said no. I meant
no. And, no, it is! Have I made myself
clear?!" He jammed his pipe hard into the

corner of his mouth, then turned on a heel and strode swiftly toward the entrance.

"Dylan?" Grace called out, hurrying after him. "Dylan wait!" Before she could catch up, Cooper was through the vestibule and charging out the door. It shut with a startling slam that stopped her in her tracks and set the bell to clanging. She stood there trying to regain her composure, the bell ringing as loudly as if a fire truck was racing past outside.

Cooper made the long journey back to his rooming house on foot only to find the door to his room had been padlocked. He slammed it against the hasp in anger, then went to the landlady's apartment and knocked on the door.

"Mr. Cooper . . . I thought you might be dropping by," she said, clearly pleased with herself. "I'm afraid you've had your last grace period. You'll have to pay what you owe or vacate the premises."

Cooper glared at her for a moment, then accepted the inevitable and nodded. "It's to be the latter, I'm afraid. If you'll be good enough to unlock the door, I'll get my things."

"Oh, you're a shrewd one, aren't you?"

she said, her voice dripping with suspicion. "But I'm no fool, Mr. Cooper. Once you 'ave your belongings, I'd never set eyes on you again, let alone the money I'm owed."

"You don't understand, my camera is in there. And I can't—"

"Is it now?" she said with a sly smile. "Fetch a pretty penny it would, I imagine. Might even fetch enough to cover what you're in arrears."

"Perhaps, it would," Cooper conceded, knowing it would fetch more, much more. "But the truth of the matter is, I can't earn a living without it; and if I can't earn a living, I'll *never* be able to pay you."

"Well, if you ask me," she said, laughing at what she was about to say. "The *real* truth of the matter is, you weren't earning one with it, either!"

Cooper took a deep breath, fighting the urge to retaliate. "Please, you have my word on it."

"It's not your word I'm after, Mr. Cooper. It's your rent. Soon as I 'ave it, you'll 'ave your camera and the rest of your belongings. In the meantime, it's out in the cold with you."

Cooper glared at her, seething, his jaw clenched with anger.

"Of course, if by some miracle you come up with your arrears, *plus* a week in advance, I'd be 'appy to let you stay on."

Miracle?! It's a miracle I haven't rung your neck! Cooper thought, resisting the impulse to do just that. "I've no belief in them. It's either luck or the lack of it."

"So true, Mr. Cooper. As they say, even a blind squirrel finds an acorn every now and then. You'll just have to get your nails dirty, now, won't you?"

Cooper's eyes flared at the insult, then softened at a sobering thought that seemed to take the steam out of him. Deep down he knew that he'd already found his acorn—*without* getting his nails dirty in the process. On the contrary, Van Dusen had actually handed it to him, but he'd given in to his pride and rejected it. He let out a long breath then smiled thinly at the landlady and said, "Aye, and even a blind beggar knows when someone's dropped a coin in his cup—unless he's deaf and dumb as well."

The landlady chuckled with glee. "Oh, that's a good one, Mr. Cooper, I'll have to remember it."

"Truth be told, lately I've been all three," Cooper said, thinking aloud as he turned and hurried down the hallway. "I'll soon be back for my belongings."

"I 'ope so, Mr. Cooper," the landlady called out after him. "But I've been running this rooming house since the summer of ninety-two, and if you come walking in here with that money, it'd be a miracle to me!"

Chapter Eight

"Bienvenue, Monsieur Cooper!" Georges Latour called out in his French accent, pronouncing it Coupaire. He sauntered down the staircase, which swept in a graceful arc from the balcony of his opulent emporium to the lobby, and shook Cooper's hand. "I'm so sorry we did not have an introduction at the Gallery Van Dusen. Now, I have the chance to say I find your work to be just superb, par excellence."

But not "excellence" enough to buy it, Cooper thought with an ironic smile. After his confrontation with his landlady, he returned to the gallery, agreed to the assignment and took an advance against it from Van Dusen, which he used to pay his rent and, much more importantly, reclaim his camera. "Aye, I'm pleased you enjoyed it. All the critics who review fine art seemed to agree. You're in good company."

"Ah, I know what you're thinking," Latour said, scolding him with a finger. "I can see it in the eyes. But just because a man appreciates something does not mean he succumbs to the temptation to possess it for his own. It's like a beautiful woman who passes you on the street. You have had such experiences, no?"

Cooper couldn't help but smile at the analogy and nodded. "Aye, more times than I can count."

"*Mais oui.* As Madame Latour often reminds me, *'Regarde, oui. Touche, non.'*"

Cooper nodded. "If there was a Madame Cooper, I'm sure she'd say the same."

"*Alors,* I'm so glad you found time in your busy schedule to come by. Monsieur Van Dusen cautioned me about getting my hopes up, but voila! Here we are!" Latour summoned two well-groomed and finely attired gentlemen, who had been keeping a discreet distance, and introduced them to Cooper as John Ogilvy and Edgar Altman, advertising and sales directors, respectively. After an exchange of pleasantries, Latour led the way up the sweeping staircase, across the polished marble floors, and through the "salles d'exposition," as he called them, where avant-garde paintings and sculptures acquired from the Van Dusen gallery were prominently displayed along with various ensembles from his collection, and where the distant strains of classical music could be heard.

En route, Cooper's head filled with the musky aroma of perfume. Was the air in the building being purposely scented? Or was Georges Latour himself trailing it in his wake. Cooper had just concluded it was the latter when Latour threw open a set of ornate doors revealing an elegantly appointed showroom beyond where equally elegantly appointed women sat on plush sofas, previewing the Latour Spring Collection. A Bach flute concerto filled the air. The music came from a Victrola atop a table that also held a large vase of freshly cut and beautifully arranged flowers. A white-gloved attendant, standing next to it, gave the Victrola an occasional crank, keeping it up to speed.

"My wealthiest and most loyal clientele," Latour whispered in an aside. "The crème de la crème of the Social Register."

The collection featured dresses with loosely draped bodices, flowing floor length skirts and wide-brimmed bonnets bedecked with flowers. As was the custom at couture houses, the ensembles were being modeled by a steady parade of mannequins.

"You see?" Latour prompted with a rhetorical flourish, addressing his clientele. "No more the waist strangling corset, no more the bustle sur la derriere, no more the rustle of the crinoline. Gone! All gone! Women are free, liberated! *This* is how ladies of the Social Register want to look while attending church services and the Easter Parade! *Très magnifique? Non*?"

While Latour played to his adoring audience, advertising director, Ogilvy, leaned to Cooper and said, "Mr. Latour means this is how they *will* want to look . . . as soon as we convince them of it."

"Aye, the power of suggestion knows no bounds."

"Exactly," Ogilvy said, smartly. "And once high society women are seen about town in these ensembles, *every* woman will want to dress as fashionably."

"But they couldn't afford to, until now," Altman explained. "Why has this changed? Because we at Georges Latour have just developed a line of similar clothing priced to fit their pocketbooks."

"And empty them as well," Cooper quipped.

"Exactement!" Latour exclaimed, rejoining them. "These advertisements—*your pictures, Coupaire*—will have *such* power of suggestion that every housewife in Boston will be at the door of Georges Latour to buy her Easter bonnet and more."

"All because of my pictures . . ." Cooper mused, emitting a stream of pipe smoke.

"But of course! As a smart gentleman Chinois once observed, each one of them will be worth a thousand words. But time is short, so, if you will leave the address of your studio with one of my assistants, the selected ensembles will be delivered within the week."

Cooper's jaw slackened. *Studio?! What studio?!* he thought, his mind racing in search of a way to avoid revealing he didn't have one. "We might just be putting the cart before the horse here," he cautioned, stalling as the pieces of a solution began falling into place.

Latour's brows knitted into a puzzled frown. "And why is this cart standing before its horse?"

"Because we're deciding where I'll be taking these pictures before deciding what we want them to express, what the power of sug-gestion should be suggesting, so to speak," Cooper replied. Then, planting the face-sav-ing idea that had dawned on him, he casually prompted, "For example, shouldn't pictures advertising the *Spring* Collection have the feeling of *springtime*, of the out of doors, of nature?"

"Absolument," Latour exclaimed, con-quered by the power of suggestion as Cooper fervently hoped. "The budding trees, the fields of flowers, the sunlight . . ."

"Aye, but there's little chance of finding *them* in my studio. No, these pictures must be taken in an outdoor setting with natural light if they're to have what you're after, if they're to fulfill the promise of the Georges Latour Spring Collection."

Latour's eyes came to life, then clouded. *"Extérieur . . . avec lumière au naturelle,"* he mused, on the horns of a dilemma. "But it is still winter. Where does one go at this time of year for trees and flowers and such?" He questioned Ogilvy and Altman with a look and received baffled shrugs in return. "You have something to propose, Coupaire?"

Cooper drew thoughtfully on his pipe as if entertaining a profound vision and nodded.

"Aye, I've been givin' it a fair bit of thought, and what keeps coming to mind is a softly focused image . . . of an elegantly dressed woman with a white parasol . . . strolling through the Botanical Gardens."

"Mon Dieu!" Latour exclaimed. "Of course, the glass-roofed pavilions, the natural light, the trees, the flowers, the sea of Easter lillies! Madame Latour herself is a member and generous contributor. A stroke of genius, Coupaire!" Altman and Ogilvy were already nodding in emphatic sales and advertising approval when Latour glanced to them and prompted, *"Par excellence! Non?"*

Cooper stifled a sigh of relief and was basking in the accolades when Latour cocked his head in thought, and said, "One last thing . . . the mannequin. As you have seen, we have many young ladies who would be happy to model for you; and as you might imagine, I have my favorites among them; but you are an artist, sir, and I have wisdom to know that an artist and his model have, as we say *en* Français, *le rapport à spécial*. I'm sure you have a special young woman with whom you always work in these situations. *Non?"*

Once again faced with being found out, Cooper thought fast, and without the slightest hesitation, replied, "Aye, I've just the lass who's perfect for it."

Chapter Nine

"Oh, no, Dylan, no, I couldn't," Grace said, her voice a mixture of embarrassment and intrigue. She and Cooper were in the North End, strolling through one of the glass-domed pavilions that were part of the Botanical Gardens. It was like being in an enchanted forest where vast beds of flowers and budding trees basked in the soft light that came through the glazed lattice-work above. "I had a feeling there was more to this than a Sunday morning stroll."

"Aye, guilty as charged," Cooper said, his burr thickening with charm. "But why not, lass? You clearly possess the necessary qualities." He picked a lily and offered it to her. "You're easily as lovely as this flower, and carry yourself in ways that go well beyond your name. There's no doubt you're perfectly suited to these pictures and this place."

Grace blushed as she took the flower and inhaled its fragrance. "As I'm afraid you can clearly see, I'm more than flattered. But a photographer's model? My brother would never allow it."

"Him again? Colin? Doubting Colin?" Cooper exclaimed, coaxing a smile out of her. "You don't seem to be the kind to cower, lass."

Grace's smile faded. Her eyes narrowed with defiance. "You know very well I'm not, Dylan Cooper."

"Aye, I know very well it's a big favor I'm asking, too, but I've no one else to turn to, Grace. Certainly not anyone with qualities such as yours."

"Mr. Latour must have dozens of models who are more than qualified. Why not employ one of them?"

"Because, despite his aversion to photography as investment grade art, Mr. Latour deigned to pronounce me an artist and, as such, assumed I have a model with whom I have a special rapport. It would've been unwise to contradict him then, and would be unwise now."

"I want to help you, Dylan, you know I do," Grace said, her voice rife with conflict.

"But you saw how Colin was at the opening. This would be a much bigger problem. I wouldn't even be here if he weren't at church this morning. Please try to understand."

"A little help would go a long way, Grace. The opening might not have been the place or the time to explain, but it seems we have both now."

Grace nodded and led the way to a bench near a pond dotted with water lillies and clusters of bullrushes. "When you decided photography would be your life's work, what was your family's reaction?"

"Well . . . ." Cooper replied, thumbing tobacco into his pipe, "they were a wee bit upset when I sold my sister's bicycle to buy my first camera."

Grace giggled like an adoring schoolgirl.

"They're just simple hardworking folks who aren't in touch with the arts," Cooper went on. "But they saw I was consumed with it and let me go my way. I guess they sensed I was put on this earth to take pictures."

"You're very fortunate," Grace said, trying not to sound envious. "My parents are simple and hardworking people, too, but, unlike yours, they have an extremely provincial view of life."

"You mean, provincial as in strict Scottish Presbyterians who believe a daughter should know her place and carry out her parents' wishes?"

"Precisely. You can imagine how they reacted when their daughter turned out to be a fiercely independent free spirit with a bent for the performing arts."

"The *performing* arts," Cooper echoed, surprised. "I thought it would be painting, sculpture, photography . . ."

"I'm taken with them all, Dylan; but I work at the gallery out of necessity, not choice. The dance has my heart. I'm classically trained."

"A ballerina," Cooper said with an amused chuckle, "which explains why you walk like a duck, doesn't it?"

Grace nodded, laughing along with him. "You know of Isadora Duncan?"

"Of course. She's famous the world over."

"Well, she was my inspiration as a child. I wanted to be just like her and dance the world over, too. So I began taking lessons in school."

"Aye, and your parents didn't think it was

a proper way for a young lady to spend her time, and they set out to crush your ambition."

Grace nodded sadly. "I'm afraid so."

"Well, don't look so gloomy, Grace," Cooper said with a jaunty cackle. "They didn't do a very good job of it, now did they?"

"No, thanks be to God. As it turned out, I was accepted by the Royal Ballet School in Edinburgh and eventually became a member of a company that performed throughout the United Kingdom. Then at the end of one season, the director announced we'd be touring America the next. That's when my parents turned over the burden of protecting my virtue to Colin. He's been my chaperone ever since."

"Now we're getting to work on the crust of the bread aren't we?" Cooper said, his eyes twinkling with understanding and delight at her rebellious nature.

"I told you it was a long story."

"So . . ." Cooper said with a thoughtful draw on his pipe, ". . . If ballet is what brought you to America, why aren't you dancing?"

"Because at the end of the tour, the booking agent stole the proceeds, and Colin and I found ourselves stranded in Boston with no way to get home."

"And your big strapping brother just let this crook get away with it without a word?"

"On the contrary, Colin confronted him; but he laughed and said a woman as pretty as I shouldn't have any trouble earning enough for two steamer tickets. You can just imagine Colin's reaction to that!"

"I daresay, I'd have bloodied the man's nose at that point," Cooper said, his fists clenched and raised like a pugilist's.

Grace nodded emphatically. "Oh, Colin did more than that! Fortunately, after all his shenanigans, the agent couldn't very well go to the police; but after Colin pounded him, neither could we, and that was the end of the money. It's been more than a year. We've been saving every spare penny for steamer tickets, but there aren't many left over at the end of the month. I barely earn enough at the gallery to make ends meet."

"I should think there'd be a place for you at the city's ballet company."

"As did I, but the few openings are given to girls from its student corps, just as we do at home. As for dancing jobs that *are* available, well, they're not the kind even a fiercely independent, free-spirited lass would consider."

"And what of Colin? He seems able-bodied enough."

"Oh, indeed, he's quite fit. Like our father and his before him, Colin went to work in the mines; but there's no coal to be mined in all of Massachusetts, let alone Boston. He took the train to Pennsylvania once, but it's just like back home there, the companies aren't hiring, they're letting people go instead."

"Aye, the lack of work is what brought so many of us here in the first place, isn't it?"

"Yes, that and now this awful war . . ."

Cooper nodded gravely. "It's a horrible situation at best. So many young men dying. Kipling's son killed, and Gladstone's grandson, too. The sons of America will soon join them, I'm afraid."

"Yes, but it's been nearly a year since Congress declared war," Grace observed. "Just the other day, I read the Europeans are asking, 'Where are the Americans'?"

"Aye, the President claims a million doughboys'll be there by summer," Cooper replied, relighting his pipe as they left the bench and strolled beneath a canopy of budding trees. "So, Grace, with things being so bad at home, why are you in such a rush to get back there?"

"Oh, I'm not sure I'm in such a rush now, Dylan," Grace replied flirtatiously. "Life seems to have taken a turn for the better as of late."

"Good, because I'm getting the feeling I'd miss you more than a little if you were to go back."

Grace smiled and lowered her eyes demurely, then cocked her head with a question. "And what about Dylan Cooper, Photographer? Was it the bad times at home that brought him to America? Or was it a sense of adventure? A burning drive to take pictures of the new world?"

"A bit of each, I imagine; but it's simpler than that," Cooper replied, emitting a stream of pipe smoke. "It was just time for a new beginning."

"Well, it will soon be that time of year, won't it? Springtime, I mean."

"Aye, but the truth of it is I much prefer autumn and winter. Something about the clarity of the light . . ."

"You know, I'm not a terribly religious person, but I always get a special feeling around Easter . . . the whole idea of it . . . especially the resurrection. I look forward to that feeling of things coming back to life. It's like having a fresh, new begining every year."

"I'm afraid it went in one ear and out the other with me," Cooper replied. "I do recall being marched into church with my class-mates on Good Friday, once; and the minister saying, 'Forgive us Jesus for crucifying thee.' Well, I said to myself this fellow's brain must have more mold than a month old haggis, because I'd nothing to do with that."

"Nor I," Grace said with a chuckle. "But Colin—now he bought it hook, line and sinker. Five minutes with him and he'll have you covinced you were the one who drove home the nails."

"He'd have little success with me."

Grace found his swagger utterly endear-ing and smiled like a student with a crush on a young professor. "So have you found it yet?"

"Have I found what yet?"

"The new beginning you came here for?"

Cooper stopped walking and captured

her eyes with his. "Oh, lately, I've a feeling I'm getting closer."

"Good," Grace said, a smile dimpling her cheeks. "Because I think I'd miss you more than a little, too."

Cooper knew she had purposely repeated his words and smiled in acknowledgement. "So, Miss Grace MacVicar from Dumbarton in the Scottish Highlands," he said, rolling his r's like thunder, "am I to take that to mean I have a mannequin for my pictures?"

Grace's eyes brightened then clouded, reflecting her conflict. "I meant it when I said I'd do anything to help you, Dylan, but I'm concerned the pleasure would be more than ruined by the pain that would be sure to follow."

"Colin."

Grace nodded. "I doubt he'd agree to it."

"Have we Doubting Grace, now, too?" Cooper teased gently. "Doubting Grace to go along with Doubting Colin? No. *He's* the one with the doubts, lass. And since I'm the one who's responsible for them, it seems it's up to me to remove them."

Chapter Ten

"Pose for fashion photographs?" Colin exclaimed, his eyes flared in condemnation at what Cooper had just proposed. He had returned from church services to the house in which he and his sister shared an apartment and found Cooper and Grace sitting on the porch. The rundown structure was located in the low-rent district of East Cambridge where the ethnic workers who serviced the local universities lived. "It's totally out of the question," Colin went on. "It wouldn't be proper for a young lady of Grace's virtue to be involved in such . . . such tawdry activities." He rapped the railing with the newspaper he was carrying and charged inside.

Grace emitted an exasperated sigh and hurried after him. "Colin? Colin I'm tried of being treated like a child."

"Then stop acting like one," Colin retorted as they entered the apartment, Cooper right behind them. "You're my younger sister and, as such, you should know your place and accept my decision." He settled in a chair and went about reading his paper as if dismissing them. The overstuffed chair was tattered and worn as were the other sparse furnishings that had come with the apartment. The uncomfortable silence was broken by the rustling of the newspaper as Colin turned the page.

"Colin? *Colin?!*" Grace said in a tone Cooper hadn't heard before. "You've no cause to be rude."

Colin lowered the paper and eyed her sullenly.

"Furthermore, I'll have none of your carping about my place, Colin. My place, which you and I know all too well, is earning enough to keep us off the dole and get us back home."

"I'll still not condone such tawdry activities."

"What activities might you be referring to, Colin?" Cooper asked, calmly, lighting his pipe. "Apparently, working in a gallery where avante-garde paintings are sold—some of them paintings of unclothed women, no less—isn't one of them."

"Grace's job is a necessary evil, which I've come to tolerate," Colin replied with an impatient snap of his newspaper. "Furthermore, Mr. Van Dusen's clients are some of Boston's most upstanding citizens. Their manners and mores are impeccable and beyond reproach."

"Aye, the very same citizens who'll be buying and wearing the clothes Grace will be modeling," Cooper concluded, smartly. "So what might you be suggesting about this that's improper, Colin?"

Colin set the paper aside and got to his feet. "You know exactly what I mean, Mr. Cooper. Throughout history artists' models have been thought of as morally corrupt women with tarnished reputations and, in my opinion, deservedly so."

"Your sister would no more partake of an activity that would corrupt her morals or tarnish her reputation than would the Blessed Virgin Mary herself."

"Yes, well, evidently you're not familiar with Grace's zeal to cavort half-naked on the stage," Colin said, his voice tinged with sanctimony.

Cooper looked aghast, incredulous. "You can't be referring to the ballet?"

"Indeed, I am. You'll not see her doing that here, I promise you, let alone pose for pictures. As those of us who work in the mines know all too well, the coal tar goes on a lot easier than it washes off. I assured my family Grace would remain . . . unsoiled . . . during our time in America and I intend to do just that."

"Of course you do, and you do it well," Cooper said, sensing the way to Colin's heart was through his ego. "You're her chaperone, Colin, and that's what a chaperone does, isn't it?"

"Well," Colin said, sounding pleasantly surprised. "I'm glad you understand."

"Aye, but do *you*?" Cooper challenged, springing the trap he'd set. "You see, Colin, human nature being what it is, some folks are eager to believe the worst of even the finest among us. So society, in its wisdom, invented the chaperone. *Not* to prohibit innocent behavior but to witness it. To testify to what *actually* happened rather than what the gossip mongers want us to believe happened. Isn't that so, Colin?"

Colin glared at him, then nodded grudgingly.

"Then do your job, Colin," Cooper exhorted. "And Grace will do hers; and I will do mine; and we'll all profit from it, and handsomely I might add."

Colin's eyes narrowed in calculation, then darted back to Cooper's. "You're suggesting it would pay well?"

Cooper allowed himself a thin smile, and nodded, emitting a stream of pipe smoke. "Aye, but I won't mislead you. If it's steamer tickets you're thinking of, it wouldn't be enough for even one; but you'd be closer to having them than you are now."

"I needn't remind you, Colin," Grace chimed in, picking up on Cooper's strategy, "as things are, we've made little headway, if any."

Colin's lips tightened, loathe to admit it, then he nodded in concession. "All right, under one condition . . ."

Grace fired an anxious glance to Cooper.

"When you've finished your work and the rotogravures are made, the negatives and prints are to be destroyed."

"Destroyed?!" Cooper exclaimed. "As conditions go that's not one I'm prone to agree to, Colin."

"Then I'm forced to withdraw my approval," Colin said with finality. "I'll not have pictures of my sister posing in clothing she would never wear, let alone afford, in the hands of people who shouldn't have them."

"I don't like what you're insinuating,"

Cooper said, on the verge of losing his temper.

Grace groaned with impatience. "What's the difference, Colin? They'll be in all the papers anyway."

"Yes, for a day, perhaps two, after which they will be discarded and this . . . this sinful interlude will have never happened."

"Sinful interlude?!" Grace erupted, losing her composure. "I'll have none of your sanctimonious posturing, Colin! Your needless opposition has only made me more of a mind to do this despite it!"

"You'd defy me though I forbade it?"

"Yes, I'm going to do this for Mr. Cooper and for us. So, you'll either be there as chaperone, or you won't. Truth be told, I'd much prefer the latter."

Colin let out an exasperated breath and glared at her. "Then I shall be there. But the negatives and prints must be destroyed, Mr. Cooper. Agreed?"

Cooper bristled at his arrogance and was on the verge of bolting when he caught sight of Grace whose eyes were pleading with him to do otherwise. He stuck his pipe hard into the corner of his mouth, then calmed himself, and grunted in the affirmative.

Chapter Eleven

Rays of filtered light were streaming through the glass-domed pavilions of the Botanical Gardens just as they were on the morning Cooper and Grace had first strolled beneath them. But now, despite the late winter chill outside—which caused the moist air in the pavilions to coat each pane with luminous condensation—the trees were exploding with foliage and the flower beds, which radiated in ever widening arcs beneath the soaring vaults of steel and glass, were fully blossoming.

Though Cooper had chafed mightily at the idea of accepting a commercial assignment, once committed, he brought all his creative powers and obsessive attention to detail to the task. After positioning Grace against a background of wisteria that cascaded from an arched trellis filtering the light, he crouched beneath the blackout cloth of his view camera, sharpening focus, adjusting perspective, and framing the composition until he had everything exactly how he wanted it—everything except its alluring mannequin.

Despite her years of training and performing on the world's stages, there was something about the camera and Cooper crouching behind it like a hunter stalking his prey that made Grace uncharacteristically self-conscious. Furthermore, every time she seemed about to overcome it, Colin, who was sitting on a nearby bench writing a letter, would look up with a disapproving gaze, and she would stiffen in disturbing contrast to the setting's serene mood and the flowing lines of the elegant couture ensemble she was modeling.

"Will you dance for me, Grace?" Cooper asked brightly, popping up like a jack-in-the-box from beneath the blackout cloth.

"Dance for you?" Grace echoed, laughing at his antics, as he intended.

"Aye. Place your trust in me, Grace, and dance," Cooper replied, waving his arms comically as if he were dancing. "It will bring out the best in you."

"Am I to dance without music?" Grace wondered, unable to contain her laughter.

"Or will you and Colin whistle a happy tune for me?"

"Oh, I suppose we could," Cooper replied with a good-natured grin. "But since I was never recruited for the choir, and Colin doesn't appear to have a happy tune in his repertoire right now, I've a better idea."

Cooper stepped to an iron-wheeled cart that he was using to move his camera gear about the grounds. It was one of several the Gardens' landscaping staff used to transport equipment and botanical specimens. A number of wooden boxes were stacked neatly on its bed. They contained sheet film, lenses, filters, tripods, and film holders. One box, with light-tight hand holes, was used to load film into the latter. Another, a well-crafted case of varnished mahogany with polished brass fittings was the box Cooper was after.

Cooper set it next to his camera and raised the lid, revealing it was a Victrola, the one from Latour's emporium. Cooper had anticipated the possibility of Grace's stage fright—or Colin fright as he thought of it—and had wisely borrowed it. After affixing the speaker horn, he slipped a record from one of the sleeves within the Victrola's base and placed it on the turntable, then gave the crank handle to Colin.

"And what am I supposed to do with this?" Colin asked, sounding offended.

"Get it up to speed, Colin, and keep it there," Cooper replied sharply. "And if you can't manage it, I'll find me an organ grinder's monkey who can."

Colin rolled his eyes and literally prayed for patience as he inserted the handle into the mechanism and began cranking. When the turntable was up to speed, he lowered the needle onto the record, and the lyrical strains of Vivaldi's Four Seasons began wafting through the beautifully landscaped pavilion.

Soon, as Cooper had expected—and eagerly awaited, for he had never seen her dance—Grace became infused with a ballerina's aura and lost in the music. His eyes crinkled with delight as she began executing rhythmic phrases of movement, seguing from petit temps lie to grand, and into a series of port de bras, then into a series of arabesques, maintaining a flowing line from toe point to fingertip. Each phrase of choreography would lead naturally to a pose that Grace would hold until she heard the click

of the shutter, then she would lyrically pirou-
ette out of it and into the next, giving each a
sense of flowing movement.

Colin looked up from his letter and
watched with a painful scowl throughout;
but, once, after Grace had performed an especially lovely pas jete, Cooper thought he
detected a thin smile of delight flickering
across her brother's tight-lipped counte-
nance.

Cooper kept it to himself and continued
taking photographs. As soon as he finished,
Grace hurried to an office in a nearby adminis-
trative building, which served as a dressing
room, to change into the next ensemble. She
had spent the previous week at Latour's emporium being attended to by a draper and a
seamstress who fitted and tailored each ensemble to her willowy figure; and they had
come along to help her change from one to
the next and assure each was properly ac-
cessorized. As soon as Grace was out of
earshot, Cooper glanced to Colin and
prompted, "Something tells me you're enjoying this a wee bit more than you thought."

"I've no idea what you're talking about,
Mr. Cooper," Colin replied, stiffly.

Cooper sighed with frustration as he

folded the tripod and shouldered the camera to move it to a new position. "Be honest with yourself, Colin. Grace is not only a most beautiful and immensely talented creature, but she's your sister as well. I caught you smiling before when she was dancing. Wasn't it because deep in your heart you take a special pride in her?"

"Deep in my heart, Mr. Cooper, I find it very hard to take pride in someone who engages in an activity of which I disapprove. That doesn't mean I'm blind to my sister's beauty and talent."

"Aye, there's hope for you yet, Colin," Cooper said with a mischievous twinkle as he set the camera down opposite the pond and secured the tripod. "I knew you were too intelligent to be equating it with the *sin* of pride—which I must admit I've been all too guilty of as of late." He ducked beneath the blackout cloth and began framing the scene on the camera's glass.

"I find neither your conceit nor rude behavior at all flattering, Mr. Cooper," Colin said, his tone sharpening. "I don't care if you think I'm intelligent or not, which I *am*; or if you think I'm a church-going prude, which I am *not*. Am I a God-fearing man?

Yes. And my faith is important to me. Of *that* I am very proud."

Cooper reappeared from beneath the blackout cloth and nodded emphatically. "And you have every right to be. I just sensed you weren't as offended by this *tawdry* activity as you'd expected."

"Make fun of me all you like, Mr. Cooper. But be warned. I love my sister very much; and I would do anything, *anything*, to ensure her safety and virtue. As for this tawdry activity, the sooner we return home the better, which as you very well know is the reason—and the only reason—I agreed to it in the first place."

"Aye, but Grace is a grown woman, Colin. Has it ever occurred to you that perhaps she's able to decide what's best for her on her own?"

"As grown as she may be, Mr. Cooper, Grace is still blissfully naive, prone to take risks, and much too willing to think the best of people. All of which, along with her goodness, makes her easy prey for the predators of this world, of which there are many."

"Aye, I thought we'd found some common ground," Cooper said with a disappointed shake of his head. "But *I* find those traits to be strengths and *you* find them weaknesses. Besides, she's not as vulnerable as you think she is; though, I daresay, with each passing day, I find myself becoming more and more deeply motivated to protect her."

"I need no help from the likes of you, Mr. Cooper."

"I wasn't offering to help, Colin, but to relieve you of the burden."

"I'm more than happy to shoulder it," Colin replied, dismayed at the sight of Grace entering the pavilion. She was wearing the next ensemble to be photographed; it featured a low, loosely draped bodice. "Besides, you've already done enough damage."

"For example?" Cooper said, sounding amused.

"That disgraceful dress Grace is wearing."

"Oh, I was thinking more of danger than disgrace, Colin, such as those predators you seemed so worried about. I can't think of any you could protect her from that I couldn't."

Colin locked his eyes onto Cooper's and said, "I can, Mr. Cooper. I can protect her from *you*."

Chapter Twelve

When the last ensemble had been photographed, Cooper retreated to his makeshift darkroom. He worked round the clock for days to develop the negatives and produce the set of prints that would be used in the newspaper advertisements; and despite their commercial end, he was bursting with pride when he and Grace, whom he insisted accompany him, delivered them.

Georges Latour, along with Altman and Ogilvy, gathered anxiously around a long table in the emporium's main salon. Cooper began laying the prints out across the expanse of polished marble; and as eager as Latour was to see them, he seemed equally intrigued by Grace's presence and couldn't take his eyes from her. "I can see why you would have *'le rapport à spécial'* with this young lady, Coupaire. If it were not for Madame Latour, I could have one myself."

"I'm more than flattered, Mr. Latour," Grace said with a winsome smile. "But, as I'm sure Madame Latour would agree, more than one *'rapport à spécial'* is one *'rapport'* too many."

"*Mon Dieu,* a sense of humor, too!" Latour exclaimed as he began circling the table, his eyes widening with delight at Cooper's pictures. *"Très magnifique, Coupaire!"* he exclaimed. *"Très, très magnifique!"*

Grace fired an excited glance at Cooper who was having little success suppressing a smile.

"They are everything I expected and more," Latour went on, the collector in him responding to their artistic excellence. "The dramatic compositions, the theatrical poses and sense of movement, the haunting diffusion of natural light—" He paused, prompting his colleagues with a look. *"Par excellence . . . Non?"*

Ogilvy and Altman exchanged anxious glances, neither wanting to be the first to say whatever had caused their foreboding silence.

"Are they not everything I say?!" Latour prompted again, unnerved by it. *"N'est pas?!"*

"Indeed they are, sir," Ogilvy finally replied. "Their artistic merit is undeniable and impressive. However, I'm concerned they will prove to be an advertising and commercial disaster."

"As am I," Altman chimed in smartly.

Latour's jaw slackened as if he'd been punched.

So did Cooper's. He shot an anxious glance to Grace who looked equally unsettled.

"Artistique?! Ou commercial?!" Latour said, throwing up his hands in frustration. "The question in the mind is: Will they, or will they not, motivate women to buy this line of clothing?"

"They will not," Altman said with unequivocal finality. "They won't generate satisfactory sales volume."

"Pourquoi?!" Latour demanded, his eyes flaring.

Altman glanced to Grace and forced a smile. "Because, with all due respect to the young lady, the mannequin is too exotic looking, too—too European."

Latour's brows twitched with confusion. *"Trop exotique?* But she is the epitome of our carriage trade clientele, and more. *N'est pas?*"

"She certainly is," Ogilvy replied. "The epitome. But these advertisements are intended to attract a different class of buyer; and those buyers are, well, less sophisticated, and more—more, for lack of a better term, full-figured women."

Altman was nodding emphatically, if grimly. "They won't be able to put themselves in the picture, so to speak, or, therefore, into the clothes."

"Furthermore, and with all due respect to the gentleman," Ogilvy said with a nod to Cooper, "these pictures are too painterly, much too . . . too museum-like. To put it bluntly, they just aren't commercial enough."

"Not commercial enough . . ." Cooper said under his breath, chewing on his pipe stem to maintain his composure.

"Yes," Ogilvy replied. "Perhaps, if I show you an example of what I have in mind?" Without waiting for a reply the suave, advertising director hurried off to one of the offices that ringed the salon. Cooper seethed, pacing like a caged animal until Ogilvy returned with a folder. He untied the ribbon and opened the flaps with a reverence that, had the folder contained Michelangelo sketches or pages from the DaVinci Codex, might have been appropriate. Cooper gave the prints a cursory inspection and scowled. "Stiffly posed, harsh lighting, pedestrian work at best."

"Exactly," Ogilvy replied. "That's exactly what we're looking for."

Latour grimaced with apprehension. "Do you think you could do something like that, Coupaire?"

"Not in a month of Sundays," Cooper replied without a flicker of hesitation. "You want to know what I really think, Mr. Latour?"

"*Mais oui,* Coupaire. I have nothing but respect for your opinion as well your talent."

"I think you hired the wrong photographer." With that Cooper swiftly gathered his prints and slipped them into the box; then, without a word, he strode out of the salon and headed down the grand staircase before Grace could stop him.

Chapter Thirteen

Cooper took the trolley back to South Boston, and headed straight for the Bonawe Furnace, a tavern just down the street from his rooming house. Named after a once legendary iron smelter in western Scotland, it served a hearty plowman's lunch, and smelled of stale beer and men who earned a living with their hands—men who gathered daily in a raucous crowd at the bar for a sandwich and midday draft.

Cooper sat alone at a table, staring into a half-empty tankard of ale that stood next to the box of rejected pictures. He'd been there about an hour when he sensed a presence and squinted through the haze to see Grace's willowy figure silhouetted against the bottle glass windows. "What brings you here, lass?" His voice had equal amounts of surprise, embarrassment, and concern. "This is no place for a lady."

"Yes, your landlady said as much," Grace replied, raising her voice above the din as she settled next to him. "I was concerned you'd be in the doldrums, Dylan. Not that you don't have a right after what happened."

"It was sweet of you to come all this way, Grace," Cooper said, touched by her gesture. "But a good wallow in them is just and proper punishment for compromising my principles, I suppose. And you, lass?"

"Well, it seems I'm no longer welcome at Monsieur Latour's emporium."

"Aye, guilt by association," Cooper concluded, feeling responsible.

"More like reckless abandon," Grace corrected with a mischievous grin. "That's what my mother would say. After you left I couldn't help but tell Latour and his minions I thought they were making a terrible mistake. He became quite unhinged and scolded me in French for what he called my *'insolence à très franche,'* which I imagine, thanks be to God, means I'll be spared further discomfort of his *'rapport à spécial'* innuendos."

Cooper chuckled heartily, envisioning the moment. "I'm sorry, I didn't mean to leave you standing there, but I'd have bloodied some noses if I hadn't." He drained the remaining ale from the tankard, then cocked his head curiously. "I thought you'd be at the gallery the rest of the day."

"As did I, but when I told Mr. Van Dusen what happened, the dear man gave me the afternoon off."

"Aye, makes two of us," Cooper said with a sarcastic cackle just as several garrulous men standing nearby burst into laughter at a joke that had just been told. One of them lost his balance and staggered backwards spilling beer across the table where Grace and Cooper were sitting. Cooper caught hold of the crude fellow just as he was about to go sprawling across Grace's lap, and helped him to his feet. "This *is* no place for a lady," Cooper said, tossing some change on the table. He tucked the box of pictures under his arm, then guided Grace through the crowd and out the door onto East Broadway, a cobbled street that ran arrow straight to the waterfront.

A brisk wind that carried a hint of spring and the fresh scent of brine was coming off the water. An armada of fishing boats returning to port extended to the horizon in a sweeping arc. Cooper and Grace walked arm in arm along the rows of slips where the vessels were docking with the day's catch.

"Lest you think I came all this way just to see if you were in the doldrums," Grace said coyly. "I've another reason as well."

Cooper gestured to some bushels of shellfish that were spilling over onto the dock. "You wouldn't have come in search of cockles and mussels alive, alive-o, now, would you?"

"Not a bad idea now that you mention it; but I came for those," Grace replied, pointing to the box of photographs he was carrying. "Latour and his fools may not want them but I do."

"And I'd like nothing better than for you to have them, Grace," Cooper said, sounding as if there was a reason she couldn't. "But what of Colin?"

Grace looked puzzled. "Colin?"

Cooper nodded. "I did promise him I'd destroy all the prints and negatives, now, didn't I?"

"Yes, I know," Grace said with a frustrated sigh. "But they're pictures of *me*, Dylan; and I want them."

"I gave my word, Grace, and I'm in the habit of keeping it."

"Yes, and an admirable habit it is, but Colin's request was terribly unreasonable; I see no reason why you should feel bound by it."

Cooper thought it over and nodded. "At best, they will be meager pay for all your hard work."

Grace studied him out of the corner of her eye. "You've no hope of being paid for yours, have you?"

Cooper shook his head no, his brow furrowing with concern. "What is it, lass? Are you in difficulty?"

"No. No, I'm fine," Grace replied, averting her eyes. "I was just wondering."

"Aye," Cooper said with understanding. "Colin will be wondering, too. Won't he?"

Grace nodded imperceptibly.

"Well, make my apologies and tell him I'll soon be back to avoiding the landlady and begging for grace periods," Cooper said, feeling lower than he had in months. "Not to mention I've no idea how I'll ever repay the advance I accepted from Mr. Van Dusen."

"He'll sell some of your pictures one day, Dylan. I know he will," Grace said, imploring him to believe it. "You can't lose faith in yourself."

"How could I with the likes of you around?" Cooper said, coaxing a smile out of her.

Grace stepped to the railing that ran along the water's edge and looked out across the harbor, her chin raised into the wind, her hair blowing in amber waves behind her, her long dress billowing like the mainsails of the ships at sea. The scene had an aesthetic and emotional power that raised Cooper's pores. He stood awestruck, feasting on it for a long moment; then, stepping closer, he put an arm around Grace's waist and tilted his head close to hers. "Can you stay with me for a while tonight, Grace?"

Grace turned to face him, her eyes filled with conflict. "Oh, Dylan, I want to," she replied, clearly torn by it. "But you know Colin will be worried. Not to mention he's expecting supper and I've yet to do my marketing."

"Aye," Cooper said forlornly. "Doubting Colin strikes again."

"Please try to understand," Grace pleaded, crushed by the disappointment in his voice. "I want to stay with you, Dylan;

and truth be told I . . . I . . ." She paused, deciding whether or not she would continue. "I know I shouldn't be so forward as to say this. Lord knows it's not at all my place, but I want to stay with you forever, Dylan; and if you're of the same mind, given time, I've no doubt I shall."

"Aye, I've plenty of time, Grace, if you're saying what I think you're saying."

"Yes, I am," Grace replied in a tender whisper. "You know, my mother used to say good things come to those who wait."

The sound of a ship's bells rode the wind as Cooper gently embraced her, holding her eyes with his. "I'd wait a lifetime for you, Grace."

"And I for you," she said softly, her eyes glistening with emotion as she caressed his face with the tips of her fingers and kissed him.

Chapter Fourteen

Dusk had fallen by the time Grace took the trolley back to Cambridge and returned to her apartment. Colin was sitting at the dining table by the window writing a letter when she came through the door with the box of Cooper's photographs and a bag that contained some cockles she'd bought while walking the waterfront with him. There was something judgmental about the way Colin held himself, she thought, as she set her things on the opposite end of the table. Since that was the rule rather than the exception, she didn't pay it any mind until she noticed the mason jar on the table next to him. It was her piggy bank. She kept it in a kitchen cupboard and, every week when she got paid, she put some money into it that Colin used at the end of the month to pay the rent. "Grace?" he called out as she slipped out of her coat and hung it in the closet. "Grace, we're short a week's rent money."

Grace nodded with apprehension. "Yes, I know. I've been meaning to talk to you about it."

"There's no time like the present, is there?" he said drumming his fingers on the tabletop.

"It's quite simple," she replied. "I didn't get paid for the week I took off from the gallery."

"I wouldn't expect Mr. Van Dusen to pay you when you weren't working," Colin said, suddenly the voice of reason. "But what of the money for your . . . your modeling work? Cooper said it would pay well."

"Yes," Grace replied, wincing at what she was about to say. "I'm afraid I didn't get paid for that, either."

Colin folded his letter as if concealing its contents from her, then set it aside and got to his feet. "Cooper didn't pay you?" he asked, sensing his low opinion of him was about to be confirmed.

"No, you see, he *couldn't* pay me, because when he delivered the prints to Mr. Latour—"

"I knew it!" Colin exclaimed, interrupting.

"He's cut from the same cloth as that crooked booking agent." He charged toward the door, rolling up his sleeves. "And he deserves the same fate!"

Grace hurried after him and caught hold of his arm as he opened the door. "No, no, wait! Listen, you don't understand. Dylan couldn't pay me because they rejected his pictures and refused to pay him."

Colin had pulled free, and was halfway out the door when Grace's words struck him. He took a moment to settle, then closed it and turned to face her. "They rejected them?" he asked, his eyes brightening. "You mean, they'll not appear in the newspapers?"

Grace nodded solemnly.

"Thanks be to God!" Colin exclaimed. "My prayers have been answered." He was enjoying the moment to the fullest when his eyes narrowed at the sight of the box on the table. "What is that, Grace?"

Grace knew all too well he meant the box of photographs, but picked up the paper bag next to it, instead. "Fresh cockles," she replied, hoping beyond hope to change the subject. "I'm going to make us a nice dinner." She took the bag and started for the kitchen without waiting for a reply.

"Not *that* Grace, *that*," Colin said, blocking her way and pointing to the box. "What is *that?*"

"A box, Colin. Just a box."

"What is *in* the box, Grace?"

"Pictures," Grace conceded, grudgingly. "The pictures Dylan took of me."

"The fashion pictures . . ."

Grace nodded.

"He gave me his word he'd destroy them."

"Yes and he intended to keep it, but I insisted otherwise."

"Why?"

"Because I wanted them."

"You wanted them?!" Colin said, raising his voice. "Well, the landlord wants the rent, Grace. I thought you were at work. Where did you find time to go all the way across town, today?"

"Mr. Van Dusen gave me the day off."

"You shirked your professional responsibilities to spend time with that shiftless photographer?"

"You sound like a jealous suitor, Colin.

You're always reminding me you're my brother, perhaps it's time I reminded *you*."

"I need no reminding, Grace. I promised Father I'd get you home safe and sound; and despite your lack of cooperation, I'll find a way to keep that promise."

"Has it ever occurred to you that I may not be going home with you, Colin?"

Colin recoiled as if slapped. "And why not?"

Grace responded with a sideways glance and a thin smile, then walked into the kitchen, carrying the bag of cockles.

Colin saw the answer in her expression and pursued her. "To take up with *him?!*" Colin demanded, beside himself. "No, no not *him!* You'll get hurt if that's what you're suggesting. I forbid it."

"I'll be fine," Grace said, taking a pot from the cupboard. "I can take care of myself."

"I know his type, Grace," Colin warned in the most foreboding tone he could manage. "He's a loner. What they call a rugged individualist. The kind of man who can't commit to a . . . a normal, stable lifestyle let alone the state of matrimony."

Grace set the pot in the sink and began filling it with water. "Matrimony?" she echoed calmly. "I didn't say anything about matrimony."

Colin emitted a relieved sigh. "Good, because there's someone at church, a gentleman who I've been meaning to introduce you to. He comes from a fine family and is a man of substance *and* means."

"I'm sure he is, Colin, and it's very thoughtful of you. But it's Mr. Cooper who has my heart."

"You're in love with him?!" Colin exclaimed, aghast at the thought. "In love with a shiftless artist?! With a man who by your own admission has no means?!"

"Such are the ways of the heart, Colin. And there's nothing you can say that will change how I feel."

"This is not acceptable, Grace," Colin protested, raising his voice. "He's too old. Too set in his ways. The man's at least forty if he's a day."

"Forty-two, actually," Grace replied undaunted. "And I'm sorry if it upsets you to hear it, but I've fallen in love with him."

Colin groaned with exasperation. "And he with you?"

"Suffice it to say, he's given me every indication of it, yes." She shut off the water, set the pot on the stove, then struck a match and lit the burner.

"Then I demand you ask Mr. Cooper if he has any intention of making an honest woman of you. If you won't, I promise you, I will."

"I *am* an honest woman, Colin," Grace protested, bristling with indignation. "And if you want some supper I suggest you refrain from implying otherwise."

"Does that mean he *hasn't* taken advantage of you?"

"No one can take advantage of me, Colin," Grace replied evenly. "And I'd have thought you of all people would know that by now."

"You still haven't answered my question, Grace."

"And I don't intend to," she said with the gentle elusiveness that he had always found frustrating. It was as if she enjoyed keeping him off balance and guessing. "It's not *my* honesty you should be questioning but your own," Grace went on, baiting him.

"Mine? What am I not being honest about?"

"About the fact that your obsession with the state of matrimony is a selfish one."

"Selfish?"

"Father would be furious if he thought you'd left me in Boston to fend for myself, wouldn't he?!"

"What's that got to do with it?"

"Be honest, Colin," she said, setting the hook she'd cast for him. "You want nothing more than to go home; and once I'm Cooper's wife, or anyone's wife for that matter, then—and only then—can you go."

"That's . . . that's . . . not   fair . . ."   Colin sputtered, stung by the truth, his hands splayed in futile objection.

Grace took the bag of cockles and dropped them into his outstreched palms. "These go in the water as soon as it starts to simmer. In the meantime, you can slice the carrots and those stalks of celery. As I said, I can care for myself. It's time you started doing the same." She strode into the parlor, took the box of photographs from the small dining table by the window and carried it to her bedroom.

She closed the door and looked about for a moment in search of a place to conceal it; then she bent to the dresser, opened one of the drawers, and slipped the box of photographs beneath some clothing. When she straightened, she caught sight of her reflection in the mirror above the dresser that revealed a profound sadness in her eyes. Colin was her brother. She loved him as he did her and she took no pleasure in hurting him; but the thought of Cooper and the feelings they'd shared that afternoon, feelings that she knew they would continue sharing for the rest of their lives, lifted her spirits and helped assuage her guilt. Maybe, she thought, just maybe, *better* things come to those who don't wait too long.

Chapter Fifteen

Easter Sunday, March 31, 1918, dawned bright and balmy along the New England coast, and the first rays of light were creeping above the rooftops as Cooper shouldered his camera and left the rooming house.

South Boston's teeming neighborhoods were always quiet at this hour on Sunday. The clatter of hooves, the rumble of internal combustion engines, the harsh cacophony of men working on the docks were all stilled. Instead, it was the smell of creosote and brine that greeted Cooper as he walked along the waterfront to the spot where he and Grace had stopped a week before. He set down his camera and looked out across the harbor, reflecting on the time they had spent there. Shafts of light were streaming between the few boats that had put to sea and, like the fingers of an outstretched hand, seemed to be offering them up to the heavens.

As the boats moved across the rising sun, Cooper quickly positioned his camera on the wood decking, then bent to the ground glass and framed his picture. Suddenly, as if someone had thrown an electric switch, the backlighting illuminated their sails like paper lanterns against the nearly black water. He was about to fire the shutter when two seagulls, which had been soaring high above, peeled off in tandem and descended toward the water. Cooper sensed what would happen and waited, firing just as the two gulls came gliding through the frame. It was a providential moment, he thought, one that captured the special feelings he and Grace had shared when they were there, and now he had captured it for her.

After packing up his camera gear, he rewarded himself with a cup of bracing black coffee and a fresh pipeful of tobacco, then bought a newspaper and sat atop the seawall reading it.

The headline proclaimed: AMERICAN CASUALTIES MOUNT. The front-page story reported that despite three years of fierce fighting on the Western Front, neither side had been able to advance. British and French forces had been bogged down in the trenches on one side of no-man's-land. The Germans had been bogged down in trenches on the other. More than three million men had been killed in this standoff. Though the United States had declared war on Germany exactly one year ago, American troops had only just begun arriving in France, albeit in huge numbers, three hundred thousand in the month of March alone. The American Expeditionary Forces, under General Pershing, were now fighting alongside the French and British to break the stalemate. More and more doughboys were among the casualties. It seemed they were being killed and wounded faster than they could be replaced, and many more recruits were needed.

The story continued inside the paper, and when Cooper turned the page, he found himself staring at a recruiting poster that depicted Uncle Sam in his star-spangled jacket and striped pants. His eyes were fixed in a fierce gaze, and his forefinger was pointing directly at the reader in intimidating confirmation of the message that—in extremely large type across the top of the poster—exclaimed: UNCLE SAM WANTS YOU!

And all other able-bodied men to sign up for military duty.

Cooper took a deep, thoughtful draw on his pipe and exhaled slowly. The wind took the smoke in a thin stream that stretched along the waterfront. He folded the newspaper and slipped it into his gadget bag, then shouldered the camera and headed back toward his rooming house where his darkroom awaited.

The city's neighborhoods had begun to come alive. Many of the residents, dressed in their Easter Sunday finery, were responding to the beckoning peal of church bells that were heralding the risen Christ.

The bells of the First Presbyterian Community Church on Auburn Street in East Cambridge were among them. It was a short walk from the apartment Grace and Colin shared, and they could feel the sound of its carillon resonating through the walls of the old house.

Colin had dressed in his Sunday best for church. He was straightening his tie when Grace emerged from her bedroom. She was wearing a floor length dress tied with a loose sash at the waist. The pale green silk was printed with a pattern of delicate spring flowers.

"Happy Easter, Grace," Colin said cheerily. "What a lovely dress. Does it mean you've decided to join me at church?"

"No, it means while I was at the salon being fitted, Mr. Latour offered me my pick of the ensembles, and I chose this one."

"Oh," Colin said, wishing he hadn't said it.

"Besides, it's too lovely a day to be indoors. I'm meeting Dylan at the Common."

"At what time?"

"About noon. Why?"

"Well, the Easter service is at ten. That would still give you plenty of time. And considering your circumstances, it's a perfect opportunity to pray for divine guidance."

"If you're referring to my feelings for Dylan, *I* believe it was divine guidance that brought us together."

"But it's Easter, Grace," Colin said, imploring her. "You've always had a special place for it. Remember when we were children we'd go to church together and buy scones afterwards on the way home?"

"We're not children anymore, Colin. Please try to remember that." Grace turned away from him and walked to the window that overlooked the street.

"Grace, please? Can't we put this contention behind us? I know we've had some difficult moments as of late, but you know I'm always well-intended."

"Yes," she sighed, sounding contrite as she turned to face him. "Truth be told, I suppose I do."

"Good, because I was thinking, since it's Easter, perhaps *we* could have a new beginning. Come to church with me, Grace? Please? I've a feeling it would give us the strength to put our differences aside." He paused and in an earnest tone, added, "And if *my* truth were to be told, nothing would make me happier."

Grace was both surprised and moved by his unabashed sincerity. She took a moment to sort out her feelings, then nodded, and in a commanding voice, said, "Under one condition—there'll be no matchmaking with any of your fellow church members from fine families with substance and means. Agreed?"

"Agreed," Colin echoed grudgingly.

"Raise your right hand," Grace commanded smartly. "Do you, Colin MacVicar, swear here and now before Almighty God to abide by this agreement, cross your heart and hope to die, with the Lord as your witness?"

Grace had recited the oath they had sworn as children, verbatim; and Colin couldn't help but picture his little sister, hands on hips, pigtails bristling, face scrunched in a pout, swearing him to do, or not do, whatever it was she wanted. The memory touched him deeply and brought a wistful smile to his face.

The flicker of joy was a welcome respite from the usual flash of anger. Grace couldn't recall when she had last seen anything remotely like it from Colin; and she was suddenly glad she had agreed to accompany him.

The First Presbyterian Community Church was crafted of stone blocks and hand-hewn timbers that had survived hundreds of harsh New England winters and a raging fire set by Redcoats during the Revolution. Beams of light shone through its stained glass windows that depicted biblical themes and scripture. Exhuberant sprays of lillies encircled the altar and the crucifix adjacent to the crow's nest pulpit. Pastor John Forsyth stood beneath its sounding board, which would project his voice to the most distant pew. His black robe displayed insignia that, to those familiar with the symbols of academia, meant he held a doctorate from the Yale Divinity School.

"Well, I see you all look stunning in your Easter attire on this most significant of Christian holidays," Pastor Forsyth began in his mellifluous baritone. "The new beginning we celebrate each year at Easter brings to mind the three women who came to Christ's tomb to find the angel who had rolled away the stone waiting for them. On seeing their profound sadness, he greeted them with the words, 'He is not here, He is risen as He said!'" Pastor Forsyth paused, his voice resonating in the hushed silence, then he repeated the angel's greeting, emphasizing each word. "And that's the real message of Easter. And when we add to that Jesus's promise, 'because I live, you too shall live,' we understand that His resurrection guarantees our own.

"Indeed, it is Christ's resurrection that makes Easter the most important of Christian holidays. For without it there would be no Christianity, no salvation and no eternal life. Most importantly, the resurrection of Jesus answers the question, Who really is Jesus Christ? In case you're wondering, He is the person who died for the sins of the whole world.

"As I look at you beautiful people today, it is hard to think of you as sinners. But as we know, the Bible says '. . . all have sinned and come short of the glory of God.' That is why Jesus sacrificed Himself on the cross and rose again three days later, so that we might have forgiveness of our sins and eternal life.

"You know, the resurrection came as no surprise to Jesus. He knew the prophets had clearly predicted it, and He went them one better. Yes, He, Himself, predicted nine times that He would rise again 'the third day.'

"As we gather here nineteen hundred years later, it's important to note that He did not rise the fourth day, or the sixth day, but the *third* day exactly as He predicted! After the resurrection, Jesus showed Himself alive to His disciples and followers for a period of forty days. Why? Because seeing the empty tomb did not turn them into believers—*seeing Christ risen did*! I'm sure you all recall Thomas, the doubting disciple, who would not believe unless he could put his fingers into the nail wounds on His hands; and then, on seeing the risen Christ, fell at His feet and worshiped Him.

"What I find incredible is that all of Christianity is built upon the resurrection of its founder. His is the only tomb in the world that is famous because it is empty. There are many tombs in this world that contain the bones of famous people. But His tomb is famous for what it does *not* contain. This is further evidence that He really did rise from the dead.

"But, you know, the Bible doesn't expect us to become believers because it says so, or even because of tradition. The prophet Isaiah said, 'Come now let us reason together saith the Lord, though your sins be as scarlet, they shall be as white as snow.' In other words, faith is not like a viral infection that strikes some people and not others. It is the result of reason based squarely on the scripture. Yes, we need to find *reasons* for believing. Here are just a few.

"The body of Jesus was never found. If it existed, surely his enemies would have used it to discredit the disciples who were preaching that he rose from the dead.

"History shows that before the resurrection of Jesus, the disciples were so timid and afraid they forsook him and fled. After they met the resurrected Christ, they were so infused by the fire of the Holy Spirit, they all became powerful evangelists.

"Their efforts to spread the word of Christ were so successful, their enemies sentenced them to death. Even as they were being executed by stoning, beheading, and crucifixion, every one of them still said Jesus rose from the dead. Would they have *all* died for a lie? Perhaps six, perhaps ten, but twelve out of twelve?!

"We owe much to those twelve men who died for the cause of Christianity; and today, we owe much to the many young men of America who have given their lives for the cause of freedom. Exactly one year ago, when this great country of ours offically entered the war in Europe, I asked you to pray for their safety. On *this* Easter Sunday, I'm asking you to pray for their souls."

Pastor Forsyth paused and bowed his head in prayer as did the congregation; then he resumed, "The simple fact that you are all here today and that you identify yourselves as Christian is evidence that you believe in Christ's resurrection. You may have been baptized as a baby, gone through confirmation, even been married in the church. But have you ever made your faith personal by inviting Christ to come into your heart to cleanse your sins and save your soul? Like doubting Thomas of old, are you willing to say to Him, You are 'my Lord and my God, this day I give my life to you'?

"Since we're commemorating our Savior's sacrifice for our sins, I'm asking you to publicly acknowledge your personal faith in Christ and His resurrection by standing in testimony of that faith." Pastor Forsyth made an uplifting gesture with his arms, bringing many members of the congregation to their feet.

Colin was among them. He had been powerfully moved by the sermon, recognizing that the pastor had been speaking about someone like *him*. Indeed, *he* had been born into a Christian family, baptized and confirmed, but had never had a personal experience of receiving Christ. Colin touched his sister's hand and smiled sweetly. "Come with me, Grace. Let's join those who are taking the Lord into their hearts."

"He *is* in my heart, Colin," Grace whispered in reply. "I've no need to make a show of it."

"I think it would be a fitting commencement to *our* new beginning to do this together, don't you?"

"Coming here with you was commencement enough, Colin," Grace replied softly.

"Please, I'm going to commit my heart to Christ, Grace, and it would make me happy if you did the same."

"I want you to be happy, Colin," Grace replied, glancing at her watch. "But my heart is committed to Dylan Cooper. And though I found the sermon eloquent and thought provoking, its duration has made me late."

Colin sighed with resignation, then walked toward the altar with other members of the congregation who had responded to Pastor Forsyth's call. For several moments, Colin knelt before the crucifix, his head bowed in prayer as the pastor asked God's blessing be bestowed upon those who had come forward. When Colin returned to the pew, Grace was gone.

Chapter Sixteen

Boston Common was a public park in the heart of downtown encircled by the wealthy enclaves of Beacon Hill and Back Bay, and the government and financial districts. The massive parcel of land was a pastoral landscape of rolling meadows, stands of lush trees, and vast plains of shrubs traversed by carriage drives and pedestrian walks. It adjoined the Botanical Gardens, which were set around a meandering lake, on the opposite side of Charles Street.

Every Easter, it seemed as if all the residents of the city made their way to the Common after church services and the Easter Parade; and it was crowded with couples strolling arm in arm, gentlemen in their Easter finery, ladies in their ensembles and bonnets; young mothers pushing prams, children playing catch, and entire families picnicking on the broad lawns.

Cooper was sitting on a bench at the west end of the lake when Grace came walking toward him aglow in her Georges Latour dress that blended with the blossoming springtime landscape.

"Happy Easter, Dylan," she called out.

"Happy Easter, lass," Cooper echoed as he got up from the bench and embraced her. Then, taking a step back, he swept his eyes over her appreciatively. "Look at you . . ." he exclaimed, starting to laugh at what he was about to say, "You're as pretty as a picture I once took."

Grace laughed along with him. "Yes, it's at home in my dresser with all the others."

"You can add this one to your collection," Cooper said, getting her undivided attention. He unfolded the newspaper and removed a print of the photograph he had taken that morning of the waterfront at sunrise. He had returned to his rooming house in plenty of time to process and print the negative prior to taking the trolley across town to the Common.

"Oh, it's lovely," Grace said, clearly moved by it.

"See?" Cooper prompted, indicating the

seagulls. "Two lovebirds soaring in the clouds. Just like us."

"You mean one's a boy gull and one's a girl?"

"Aye, that they are."

"I can't imagine how you can tell?"

"Well, I'm sure we can agree that, like you, this one is obviously the younger and more beautiful of the two, and is therefore the girl."

"Obviously . . ."

"By the process of elimination," Cooper went on, "the other weather-beaten one with the scarred beak and the ruffled feathers, like me, must be the boy."

"Beauty and the beast, is that it?" Grace teased.

"Perhaps we can be a bit more charitable than that. How about beauty and the chap with the finely chiseled—"

"Beauty and the old warhorse?" she interrupted, bursting into laughter.

Cooper laughed along with her, then his expression darkened. "There won't be many of them around after this war, I'm afraid. Have you seen the paper?" He held it up displaying the headline.

Grace winced at its message. "No, but

the pastor spoke of it this morning," she replied sadly. "It was a very moving sermon."

"You attended an Easter service?" Cooper said momentarily surprised. "Ah, Colin, I suppose."

"Yes, he really wanted me to accompany him. I just couldn't say no. Actually, I'm glad I went."

Cooper nodded, offered her his arm and they began walking along the edge of the lake. She in her Georges Latour ensemble, he in his tweed jacket, plaid shirt, and worn corduroys, somehow in perfect compliment and contrast. They had gone a distance around the curving bank when they stopped to watch some children sailing toy boats. Cooper lit his pipe and tossed the flaming match into the water, then glanced over at Grace. "So, is he going to sign up?" he prompted, broaching the subject, obliquely.

"Colin? For the military?"

Cooper exhaled a stream of smoke and nodded.

"I don't know. He's never said anything about—" She paused as the real reason Cooper had asked suddenly dawned on her.

"Oh dear, Dylan, please tell me you haven't."

"I haven't."

"Oh," she sighed, relieved. "Thanks be to God."

"But I feel a strong obligation," Cooper confided. "I've not one country to serve, Grace, but two."

Grace's posture slackened. "But why? Just when we're starting to see a life together . . ."

Cooper's eyes softened with empathy. "I know, lass. It's been weighing on me all morning."

"It's just not fair."

"Aye, not a'tall," Cooper said, visibly distraught. "The trouble is the Germans have not only taken Belgium and invaded France, but, according to the paper, they have far grander designs."

"Yes, everyone's saying Great Britain will be next. Despite the Channel, Calais is still closer to London than Paris. Isn't it?"

"Aye, I'm afraid so. They have to be stopped. If everyone turns a deaf ear, they'll overrun the whole of Europe. Look!" He tapped the newspaper headline with the stem of his pipe. "Young Americans are giving their lives for *us*, Grace. They're dying to protect your family and mine. How could I fail to sign up?"

Grace lunged into his arms, hugging him tightly. "Oh, I know you're right," she said in an anxious whisper. "I'm afraid your sense of duty only makes me love you more." She tightened her grasp, then leaned away slightly and looked up into his eyes. "I don't want to be a lone seagull, Dylan. I've been one for too long."

"As have I," Cooper said softly, embracing her.

They spent the remainder of the afternoon together in the Common, holding hands and embracing more than they spoke, for there was little left to be said other than the heartfelt expressions of affection and emotion they shared; and there was a haunting sadness in their eyes when they parted.

"I'll wait a lifetime for you, Dylan," Grace said, kissing him for what might be the last time.

"And I for you," Cooper said, softly, when their lips reluctantly parted.

Chapter Seventeen

Early the next morning, Cooper went to the Army Induction Center in the Federal Building on Congress Street. He joined the line of enlistees that already extended out the door, down the steps, and across the pavement to the corner and beyond. Some of the faces were filled with the eager innocence of boys still in their teens, others were etched with the weary concern of men well past middle age.

Several hours later, Cooper found himself in a massive assembly hall. Long tables ran in parallel rows across the cavernous space where hundreds of men sat filling out registration forms.

In the box labeled Occupation, Cooper wrote: *Photographer*. Though he assigned no special significance to it, the officer who reviewed his paperwork took note of it. Seated behind one of the many processing desks that ringed the hall, he wore a crisply pressed uniform with Captain's bars on the epaulets and a field of campaign ribbons and medals carefully arranged above the left breast pocket. "Take a seat," he said as he looked up from the forms Cooper had filled out. "So, you're a professional photographer, Mr. Cooper?"

"I'm an artist," Cooper replied, sitting upright in the chair. "I don't take commercial assignments."

"But you're professionally trained. It says here you attended the University of Glasgow."

"Aye, the School of Technical Arts, they called it," Cooper said with a disdainful scowl.

"But you didn't matriculate . . ."

"I ran out of funds, I'm afraid."

The Captain smiled knowingly. "I'd have given anything to have had someone like you in my unit when I was over there."

Cooper looked puzzled. "What could *I* have done that any of the others couldn't?"

"Field intelligence," the Captain replied smartly. "I used to play cards with an officer who was heading up an Air Force squadron at the time. Bright fellow. Always thinking.

Well, he had this idea to take pictures of enemy troop emplacements."

Cooper's eyes widened with intrigue. "You mean, he wanted to take a camera up in a plane and take pictures of the ground."

"Exactly. I thought it quite clever, too," the Captain said, seeing Cooper's reaction. "He called it aerial reconaissance. Sixty-three of my men would still be alive if you, or someone like you, had been there."

Cooper's jaw dropped. "Sixty-three?" he repeated in an incredulous whisper.

The Captain nodded grimly. "We were trying to evacuate some wounded from a ravine and got caught in a crossfire. We had no way of knowing there were enemy machine-gun positions above us on both sides. It was like shooting fish in a barrel. A bloodbath. Just one aerial picture would've . . ." He let the sentence fade off with a grimace, then slipped Cooper's paperwork into a file folder and printed his name on it. "Get in that line for your physical," he said, gesturing to it with the folder. "The doc'll have this by the time you reach him."

Cooper nodded tight-lipped and got to his feet. He was about to leave when the Captain pushed back in his chair and did the same. Cooper recoiled slightly, his eyes widening in shock at what the desk had, up to this moment, concealed: The Captain was standing on one leg. The other had been amputated above the knee and the lower half of his pants was pinned up against his thigh. Cooper was momentarily paralyzed, neither able to speak nor move. The Captain fetched a pair of crutches that was leaning in the corner behind his desk and set them under his arms, then noticed Cooper standing there slack jawed. "Get in that line," the Captain commanded.

The officer's sharp tone pulled Cooper out of it and sent him hurrying across the hall. From the end of the long queue, Cooper watched as the Captain secured his file folder in the Y of one of his crutches, then made his way on them to a nearby office. The door was open and another officer came from behind his desk to join the Captain who opened Cooper's folder and began gesturing to its contents, animatedly, as he spoke.

In the military, the joke was that truck drivers ended up as clerks, clerks ended up as pilots, and pilots ended up as truck drivers. At least for the moment, it seemed to

Cooper that a photographer might just end up as a photographer with a chance to save lives rather than take them; and the possibility propelled him through the remainder of the induction process with a clear sense of purpose and resolve.

Chapter Eighteen

Grace spent the day at the gallery, trying to lose herself in work, but she couldn't stop thinking about Cooper. Would she see him again before he went off to war? Would she ever see him again at all? Try as she might, she couldn't keep her mind on the paintings she was cataloguing, and when Van Dusen discovered an error, she apologized and confided in him. Despite his efforts throughout the day to lift her spirits, she was still out of sorts when she returned home that evening.

After dinner, Grace settled with the evening paper beneath the glow of a flickering gaslight; and like a moth to a flame, read every word of every story that had anything to do with the war in Europe, which further unsettled her.

"You're awfully quiet, Grace," Colin prompted. He signed a letter he had been writing, then slipped it into an envelope and addressed it.

"I should think you'd be pleased," Grace said from behind the newspaper.

"So would the family," Colin teased. "I sent them your love. I hope you don't mind?"

"Not at all. Though I should think they've more than enough of it with all the letters you send."

Colin forced a smile, then crossed to the closet and slipped the envelope into a pocket in his coat. "You know, whenever you get like this it's because you're unhappy about something." He hooked a finger in the fold of the newspaper, peering over the top of it at her. "And though I don't approve of your seeing Cooper, I must admit it's made you quite the opposite. So I can only conclude you've had some sort of a spat."

"Well, your conclusion is incorrect," Grace retorted with a dismissive snap of the newspaper.

"Very well, but knowing you as I do, I'm quite certain it has something to do with him."

"What if it does?" Grace said, remaining

hidden behind the newspaper. "It's still no business of yours."

"I'm your brother Grace. If he's done something that's made you unhappy, well, I think—"

"He enlisted today," Grace interrupted sharply. She lowered the newspaper and glared at him.

"Really? Enlisted?" Colin echoed, brightening; then laughing at what he was about to say next, added, "Oh, I wouldn't be concerned if I were you, Grace. They're looking for men, not *old* men."

"That's not funny, Colin," Grace protested. "As a matter of fact it's horrid and . . . and uncharitable. I don't see *you* enlisting."

"*I'm* not faced with the looming prospect of making a lifetime commitment to a young lady, now, am I?"

Grace tossed the paper aside and leapt from the chair. "How dare you suggest Dylan would enlist merely to avoid the . . . the 'state of matrimony' as you call it."

"No need to get so upset, Grace," Colin counseled coolly. "As you might imagine, I'm glad to be rid of him, whatever his reasons."

Grace's face reddened with anger. "I've put no pressure on Dylan. None whatsoever, and you know it. Being together is all that matters to me."

"Please," Colin said, rolling his eyes. "No need to remind me. These things have a way of working out for the best. You'll see."

"He's a good man, a courageous man," Grace went on in passionate defense of Cooper. "I'm going to miss him terribly."

"You have your opinion of him and I have mine," Colin said in his haughty way, which further incensed her. "If you ask me, I think the war appeals more to his sense of adventure than his sense of patriotism."

"You can't bring yourself to admit he's well-motivated, can you, Colin?"

Colin folded his arms and shook his head with dismay. "You know, Grace, it's very disappointing that we still haven't found a way to air our differences without you getting so worked up over them."

"*You're* the one who gets worked up, Colin," Grace retorted, jabbing a finger at him. "I've grown weary of your incessant antagonism. This new beginning, which you pined for, is turning out to be terribly one-sided."

"I care about what's best for you, Grace, and—" Several sharp raps on the door interrupted him, indeed startled him since he was standing next to it. Colin undid the latch, then opened the door and groaned at the sight of Cooper standing in the hallway. "I told you he was a bad penny, Grace."

Grace nearly knocked Colin over as she dashed across the room. "Dylan?" she exclaimed, looking as confused as she did excited as he stepped inside and closed the door. "I was afraid you'd be sent off for training immediately. How long have we before you're to report?"

A funny smile broke across Cooper's face. "We've a lifetime, Grace."

"A lifetime? I don't understand."

"They turned me down."

Colin sighed like a deflating balloon.

Grace lunged into Cooper's arms bursting with joy. "I'll put up some water for tea," she said, calling back over her shoulder as she headed into the kitchen. "I don't know whether to cheer or cry."

"So what was it," Colin asked, rhetorically. "Poor vision, flat feet or . . . your artistic bent?"

Cooper glared at him, angered by the innuendo. "Be advised, Colin, it was my artistic bent that caused them to consider me at all!"

"I see. So then what was it that ultimately did you in?"

Cooper seethed, loathed to reveal the reason. "My age," he finally replied, unable to conceal his chagrin and disappointment. "The limit is thirty for general conscripts and, in my case, forty for technical specialists."

"Did you hear that, Grace?" Colin prompted, trumpeting his Pyrrhic victory. "I told you."

"You certainly did, Colin!" Grace said, her voice ringing with unbridled enthusiasm and an equal measure of sarcasm. "Things do have a way of working out, don't they?"

And in the weeks that followed, they did. Grace spent her days at the gallery and Cooper went camping. Not because he was in need of solitude and soul-searching as he had been earlier, but because he needed to throw himself into his work.

Venturing off alone on a photographic expedition, he took the train that ran along the coast to the fishing village of Gloucester about thirty miles north of Boston. Camera and tripod balancing on one shoulder, gadget bag and survival gear hanging from the other, Cooper spent weeks exploring and photographing the area. He hiked vast distances one day and, coming upon something of visual intrigue, stayed put the next. But it was the village of Newbury, nestled in a cove just south of the New Hampshire line, that inspired him beyond anything he had seen. Taken by its dense wilderness, rugged coastline, small town charm and hearty people, all of which powerfully reminded him of home, he remained there taking pictures until he ran out of film.

Cooper returned to Boston immediately and spent the next week in his makeshift darkroom processing and printing the negatives. When finished, he took the trolley across town to the Van Dusen gallery and surprised Grace.

"I've no appointment I'm afraid," Cooper said with a grin, handing her a box of prints.

"I'll have to clear it with Mr. Van Dusen," she said, playing along, before erupting with delight at the sight of him. Cooper enfolded her in his arms, holding her tightly, his head swimming with the scent of her perfume. When he finally released her, she took a moment to catch her breath and straighten her clothing. Then she opened the box and began sorting through the prints. Her eyes were soon sparkling with delight at what they beheld. "Oh, Dylan, they're breathtaking. Just breathtaking. They have something special, extra special."

"Aye, I've had the same feeling for weeks."

"And these . . ." Grace paused and sorted through the prints again, this time culling out the ones of Newbury. "These remind me so much of home."

"I knew they would, lass," Cooper said, his eyes aglow at sharing it with her. "I had the same reaction. Newbury. Just up the coast a ways."

"You must take me there one day. Will you?"

"Of course, lass."

"Promise?"

Cooper responded with an emphatic nod. "We'll need to get some proper transportation first. It took me a week to get there and a week back with a lot of camping out along the way."

"Oh, I can't wait for Mr. Van Dusen to see these!" Grace exclaimed, spacing out the prints on the long table. She selected one—a picture of a wave smashing against a rock formation filling the air with sparkling droplets of water—and set it on the easel, then hurried off to fetch Van Dusen from a back room where paintings were stored in racks that went from floor to ceiling.

"Good to see you, Cooper," Van Dusen said with an enthusiastic handshake. "Grace seems to think you've outdone yourself." He stepped to the table and swept his eyes over the photographs, his head nodding, tilting, bobbing in agreement at each and every one. "Indeed, up to your standard and beyond," Van Dusen said, his voice breaking with emotion at the sight of the print on the easel. "Oh, yes, breathtaking to be sure. Your time will come, Cooper. I've no doubt of it."

Cooper's brows arched with uncertainty. "Aye, but I'm getting the feeling that as far as the Van Dusen gallery is concerned, it hasn't come yet, has it?"

"I'm afraid not," Van Dusen replied with a sigh. "The war has had an enormously depressive affect on the art market. My clientele are more risk averse than ever. They aren't buying much of anything. I suspect the only thing they're investing in these days is gold."

"Well, they won't go to waste," Cooper said sarcastically. "I'll put them away and burn them next winter for warmth."

Van Dusen's head tilted as if struck by a thought. "I wouldn't do that if I were you."

"And why not?"

"Because someone who might be interested in them, perhaps in all of them, just came to mind," Van Dusen replied with growing excitement.

"All of them?" Cooper echoed, astounded.

Van Dusen nodded, then turned to a bookcase and began searching for something.

"One or two would be sufficient," Cooper went on. "But dozens? I'd be a fool to believe it, and they'd be fools to do it."

"Fools or not, they've been around since the late eighties, if I recall correctly," Van Dusen replied, looking through the publications on the shelf. "Here we are . . ." He pulled a thick pamphlet from between some books and handed it to Cooper. It had a bright yellow border and large typography that proclaimed: The National Geographic Society. "You familiar with them?"

"Nope, can't say that I am," Cooper replied, as he thumbed through it and the pages of black and white photographs it contained.

"Well, it came recently," Van Dusen explained. "It seems they're soliciting material: scholarly writings, photographs. The Society also funds geographic explorations. They subscribed a substantial sum to Admiral Peary's expeditions to the North Pole."

"This is high quality work," Cooper said, clearly impressed by the pictures in the pamphlet. "Very high quality work. All of it."

Van Dusen nodded and took the pamphlet from Cooper. "And as I recall, they reward it with high quality pay." He turned to the inside of the front cover, scanning it until he found what he was after, then read aloud, "'Organized for the increase and diffusion of geographic knowledge. Articles and photographs are desired. For material which the Society can use . . . *generous remuneration is made*.'"

"For material which the Society can *use*," Cooper admonished. "With my luck, they won't be remunerating me for my pictures, they'll just be returning them."

"Perhaps," Grace chimed in. "But as a soon to be famous photographer once said . . . 'There's only one way to find out,' isn't there?"

"You're just all sugar and spice and everything nice, aren't you, lass?" Cooper teased in response to her using his own argument against him.

"I wouldn't count on everything nice," Grace retorted with a mischievous grin.

"I suppose I could settle for two out of three," Cooper said, matching it. "But I'm afraid you're both forgetting that soon to be famous photographer found out something he didn't want to find out."

Despite his skepticism, with Grace's assistance, Cooper selected and packaged several dozen prints between sheets of cardboard in an envelope that she addressed to the National Geographic Society, Hubbard Memorial Hall, Washington D.C. As the pamphlet instructed, Cooper included a similar self-addressed, stamped envelope in which rejected material would be returned. He also included a sheet of paper on which he wrote: *Might you be able to use any of these?* And signed his name.

"I've got a good feeling about this," Van Dusen said as they sealed the envelope.

"So do I," Grace said. "Dylan's time has come."

"Well," Cooper said with a wiley smile, "I'm *tempted* to agree. But I've learned from bitter experience not to trust it."

Chapter Nineteen

"Mr. Cooper? Mr. Cooper?" the landlady called out. Cooper had just returned to the rooming house after a sandwich and midday draft at the Bonawe Furnace when she came running down the corridor after him. "I have something for you, Mr. Cooper. Came this morning," she went on, waving an envelope at him, which she seemed intent on retaining. "I can't imagine why some society, in Washington D.C. no less, would be sending post to the likes of you?"

Weeks had passed since Cooper had mailed his photographs to The National Geographic Society. One look at the envelope, which the landlady finally relinquished, set his heart to pounding. He had no doubt it was the self-addressed, stamped envelope he had included at the Society's request; but it was as thin as if it were empty; and obviously hadn't been used to return the prints he had sent them.

Instead, it contained a one page letter on the Society's beautifully engraved stationery. Its well-crafted paragraphs of praise, encouragement, and interest in acquiring more of Cooper's work left no doubt that Van Dusen was right! The National Geographic Society had bought every one of Cooper's photographs; and, as the enclosed check confirmed, it meant every word of its offer, because the amount more than qualified as "generous remuneration."

Cooper had never had enough money, let alone *extra* money, and therefore never needed a safe place to keep it; but having suddenly acquired both, he opened a savings account at South Boston Savings and Loan on Dorchester Street. The next thing he did was pay back Van Dusen the advance he had taken against the Latour assignment.

After so many years of struggling to make ends meet, Cooper wanted to enjoy the sense of security his windfall provided, not squander it; but there was something he had always wanted. It would be useful in his work and would require he expend but a small percentage of his funds. He considered having Grace come along to advise him on the purchase, but decided to surprise her instead, and made it on his own.

The next day was Saturday. Cooper and Grace had been spending weekends together and this one would be the same— with one exception. He paid the landlady for the use of the rooming house phone and placed a call to the gallery. When Grace answered, Cooper suggested that rather than meeting at her apartment—as was their habit before going off into the city—they meet at the trolley stop down the street instead. To Grace's bemusement and intrigue, he humorously refused to divulge the reason.

Grace was there at the appointed hour, expecting Cooper to get off the trolley or come sauntering around the corner at any moment; but a half hour later, there still wasn't any sign of him. She was about to leave when the incessant honking of a horn got her attention. She turned in the direction of the sound and saw a gray pickup truck barrelling down the street toward her.

Cooper was behind the wheel, depressing the horn with one hand and waving out the window with the other.

The truck ground to a stop beside Grace with a chilling screech of its mechanical brakes. It had a two-passenger cab and an enclosed cargo bed in which Cooper's camera, tripod, and boxes of gear were secured. The fenders were dinged and the running boards were worn, but it had a sturdy look to it and the engine seeemed to be running with surprising smoothness.

"What's this?" Grace asked with astonishment.

"A proper mode of transportation," Cooper replied with a jaunty air. He reached across the seat and unlatched the passenger door, letting it swing open. "Climb aboard, lass. We're going for a ride!"

"Newbury?" Grace prompted with hope and excitement in her voice.

"Aye, Newbury it is." He put the truck in gear and drove off. "Sorry to be so tardy, but the engine refused to turn over. I suppose it's going to take me awhile to get the hang of cranking it."

"I'm sure you'll get the 'hang' of it," Grace said with a laugh, mimmicking him as he made the turn onto Main Street, which ran arrow straight to the Longfellow Bridge, depositing them in the North End. Cooper negotiated the knot of interconnecting roads taking Route 1, the Boston Post Road, the main coastal highway that ran north from New York through Connecticut and Massachusetts to the New Hampshire line and beyond.

Still, it took over two hours to cover the forty miles to Newbury. Finally, the quaint, small town architecture and shop-lined streets that fanned out from its snug harbor where a small armada of vessels bobbed at anchor, came into view.

Grace could hardly contain her excitement at the sight of it, which raised her pores. "Oh, it is so much like home, Dylan! I can hardly believe it!"

"Nor I," Cooper said, equally enthused. "I've a feeling that I could spend the rest of my days here."

He and Grace spent the day exploring the town and surrounding area. They drove past the shops on Sycamore Street where a youngster, named Joe Clements, was sweeping the sidewalk in front of his father's printing shop; and had an impromptu lunch—of bread, cheese and wine—on a rock jetty that swept out into the placid waters of Newbury Cove. Far below, sixth-grader Alicia Johnson, her fists locked around the oars of a bobbing dinghy, was being taught to row by her father.

It was mid-afternoon when Cooper pulled into the one-pump gas station where a sign proclaimed: GAS 8¢ GA, and asked the proprietor, an older fellow in a pair of grease-smudged coveralls, to fill the tank.

"Look at that," Grace said, pointing to another sign, this one in the station's window, which advertised: Cottage For Sale $1,200.

Cooper shrugged. "What of it?"

"I think we should inquire about it."

"Why?"

"I don't know. Just a feeling, I guess. Aren't you the one who said you could spend the rest of your days here?"

"Aye, but not by spending my last penny to do it," Cooper replied. "I came here intending to buy a few gallons of gasoline, Grace, not a cottage."

"I know, but sometimes things happen for a reason, Dylan," she said with a playful wiggle of her brows. "It seems almost providential if you ask me."

"You're starting to sound like Colin, if you

ask *me*," Cooper joked. "It will be the most expensive fill up this fellow's ever had."

"Why don't you find out where it is?"

Cooper grimaced.

"*I'll* ask him, all right?" Grace got out of the cab without waiting for an answer and approached the old fellow who was filling the tank.

"It's just a short drive up the coast," he replied to Grace's query. "Up on a hill, view of the harbor, property's real nice, too." He went on to explain he had put the cottage up for sale because his children had grown and were long gone and he and his wife had recently moved into town. "Got the keys right here." He slipped them from a pocket in his coveralls and handed them to Grace, then sketched a map and jotted a few directions on a slip of paper she took from her handbag. "It needs some work, but you'll see it's worth the price. Of course, if a nice young couple really wanted it . . ." He let it trail off with its implication, then pulled the nozzle from the fill pipe and hung it on the pump. "Twelve and a half gallons," he said to Cooper, stepping to the driver's side window, "makes it exactly a dollar. No charge for directions," he added jovially.

Cooper's brow furrowed with confusion. He swung a look to Grace who had gotten back into the cab and was settling next to him. "Directions to where?"

"To a new beginning," Grace replied, displaying the slip of paper and the keys to the cottage, which were dangling inches from Cooper's nose on the ring she held between thumb and forefinger.

Chapter Twenty

A short time later, Cooper was guiding the pickup through the twisting turns of the two-lane blacktop that snaked along the coastline. Waves were smashing against the craggy rocks, sending up sprays of water that spattered across the windshield.

"There should be a dirt road coming up on the right," Grace said, navigating from the map.

Cooper found it and made the turn. The unpaved road climbed a steep hill, then flattened out across a plateau at the summit; and there, beneath a stand of trees that were bending in the wind, stood a weathered cottage. Rambling was the adjective that best described its architectural style. Indeed, it appeared as if it had grown this way and that, a room at time with little regard for what had gone before, producing a meandering floor plan and mismatched rooflines.

Grace thought it seemed perfectly suited to Cooper's bohemian style and serendipitous character. "It's wonderful," she exclaimed as they left the pickup truck and walked the grounds. "It's so much like you, Dylan."

"It's also twelve hundred dollars," Cooper protested, though he was already eyeing the double-width garage. He thought it would make a perfect darkroom. "That's a lot of money, Grace. Almost six times what I paid for my truck."

"I've a feeling the price might be open to negotiation," Grace said, recalling what the old fellow had implied.

"Perhaps, but there still wouldn't be much left from what the Society paid for my pictures."

"Didn't their letter say they were interested in purchasing more of them?"

"Aye, but I don't know if I'd be wise to trust it, lass. Truth be told I want to, but . . ."

"Then trust it, Dylan," Grace said in her spirited way. "Take a chance."

Cooper winced with uncertainty. "I don't know, I'm finally feeling a bit secure—just a *wee* bit mind you. But it's no time to be feeling my oats and turning into a spendthrift. Though Lord knows it's tempting . . ."

"Some temptations are worth the risk, remember?" Grace prompted with as much spunk as she could muster. "I'll take it with you. We could be happy here, Dylan. I know we could."

"Aye, it does feel a whole lot like home doesn't it?" Cooper said, sweeping his eyes over the vista.

Grace nodded emphatically. "It gives me a feeling of comfort and sense of belonging," she said, her eyes brightening with an idea. "Maybe you should take some pictures of the place? We could show them to Mr. Van Dusen and see what he thinks."

"That's a fine idea, lass," Cooper said, wasting no time unloading his gear from the back of the pickup.

While he went about photographing the cottage and grounds, Grace went inside. The kitchen had serviceable appliances along with ample closets and cupboards. There was a large stone fireplace in the parlor, and an atrium where the disparate wings of the cottage intersected. It was capped by a skylight beneath which Grace imagined a botanical garden of potted plants would thrive. She continued to tour the other rooms, thinking about how they might be furnished, and entertaining thoughts of curtains, throw rugs, and other homey touches.

A short time later, Cooper had the camera trained on the front of the cottage. He was on the verge of firing the shutter when the screen door swung open and Grace emerged from within. Cooper paused, waiting until she was right where he wanted her in the composition, then fired it.

"Oh, I hope I didn't spoil your picture."

"Nope, I only fire the shutter when I want to."

"I suppose I should know that by now, shouldn't I?" Grace said, laughing at herself. She walked to a corner of the cottage and gestured to the windows that overlooked the sea. "It seems this room gets the morning sun," she said with a coy smile. "It would make a perfect nursery."

"Nursery?" Cooper echoed, a broad grin breaking across his face. "I think we'd best own the place before we start filling it with little ones, don't you?"

"Does that mean you've decided to purchase it?"

An impish smile broke across Cooper's

face. "I'm so inclined, aye. But I thought we were going to get Mr. Van Dusen's opinion first." He tilted his head with uncertainty and lit his pipe. "Come to think of it, we might be wise to consider what Colin might have to say about it, too."

"Colin?" Grace echoed with a puzzled expression. "I don't see the value of his opinion in this matter."

"I'm afraid I didn't make myself clear, Grace," Cooper said, drawing on his pipe. "I meant, what would he be thinking if you and I left Boston and moved up here together?"

"You know very well he'd pronounce me a wanton woman living in sin, and forbid it with his customary histrionics."

Cooper nodded, emitting a stream of pipe smoke. "It's a matter of some concern, isn't it?"

Grace's lips tightened with defiance. "Not to me. I just want to be with you, Dylan. *Here* with you, together for the rest of our lives."

"Aye, as do I," Cooper said, a grin tugging at a corner of his mouth at what he was about to say. "Of course, there is one thing we could do that would forever end Colin's histrionics, isn't there?"

Grace cocked her head, eyeing him with suspicion. "Might you be saying what I think you're saying?"

Cooper smiled enigmatically and guided her to a weathered bench that had been positioned on the bluff to take full advantage of the view. The late afternoon golden light made the cottage appear to glow from within, and the breeze coming off the water filled the air with the salty scent of brine. When Grace was comfortably seated, Cooper took her hand in his and dropped to a knee. "I'm saying, I want you to marry me, Grace."

Grace seemed stunned by his proposal, but it was actually a disturbing thought that had silenced her. "Why?" she finally responded. "Because it would make Colin happy? I can't think of a worse reason, I'm afraid."

"No, to make *me* happy, Grace," Cooper replied with utmost sincerity. "You have my heart, lass, and always will," he went on, pressing her palm to his chest. "Every beat that's left in it is yours and yours alone. And I want you . . . and the little ones that'll be in that nursery one day . . . to have my name."

He paused, an uncertain look crinkling his eyes. "I thought you wanted the same."

Grace's eyes filled with remorse. "I'm sorry, I didn't mean to sound so harsh. I guess I'm just tired of always worrying about what Colin will think, or what Colin will say, or what—"

"Shush lass," Cooper said, putting a finger to her lips, silencing her. "No need for any of that. A simple yes or no answer will suffice."

Grace nodded, her eyes glistening with emotion. "Yes . . . I'll marry you. Truth be told, I'd have agreed to it the morning you first walked into the gallery."

Chapter Twenty-One

Several months had passed. Summer warmth had come to New England, bathing its endless miles of coastline in golden sunshine and making its vast forests lush with verdant foliage and vegetation.

After seeing the photographs of the cottage, Van Dusen conferred with a real estate broker he knew well and trusted. The broker agreed that the cottage would be an excellent investment and encouraged Cooper to purchase it. As Grace had surmised, the price was more than negotiable, and when all was said and done, Cooper had paid the proprietor of Newbury's one-pump gas station the unnerving sum of one thousand dollars for it.

Despite his initial anxiety, buying the cottage turned out to be a providential event that had a positive effect on everyone connected to it, and suddenly life was good.

The National Geographic Society had been making regular purchases of Cooper's photographs, providing him with steady income. Grace and Colin had made their new beginning, which was really a resumption of the more playful, less contentious brother-sister relationship of their childhood. Colin had come to accept Cooper as the man who would be his sister's husband and was pleased they were making plans to marry and settle down in the cottage.

Cooper had wasted no time moving out of the rooming house in South Boston and into the cottage. He immediately went about tackling the long list of badly needed repairs, and, most importantly, turning the garage into a darkroom. He blacked out the windows, built storage racks and work surfaces, and ran in electrical and plumbing lines, then installed a sink, and a cast-iron stove to keep him and the chemicals he used to process photographs from freezing in winter.

Occasionally on weekends, Cooper would drive down to Boston in his pickup to shop for furnishings with Grace; but, most often, she and Colin would take the train to Newbury, giving Grace the opportunity to nest and bring a woman's touch to the cottage's many rooms; and give Colin the opportunity to help Cooper with the repairs. With the cause of their friction removed, they had come to like each other, bonding over the manly endeavors of carpentry, painting, plumbing, roofing, and brush clearing. As soon as Grace had the kitchen up and running, they cleared out an area in a grove of trees where they set up a table and chairs. The three of them often ate in the leafy shade, cooled by the breezes that came off the sea.

As part of their commitment to their new community, Grace and Cooper decided to be married in the Newbury Presbyterian Church—a white clapboard structure with a soaring steeple that stood on the town square. Colin had been attending Sunday services when in Newbury and was put in charge of making the wedding arrangements with Pastor Martin Surtees who would perform the ceremony. A date had been set. Grace was sending out invitations; Cooper was shopping for a ring.

One sweltering Saturday, as he did every day after lunch, Cooper headed down to the row of mailboxes at the end of the dirt road to collect the newpaper and post. There was rarely any of the latter, and today was no exception. He removed the newspaper, immediately unfolding it to read the headline and scan the front page stories as he walked back to the cottage. A letter-sized manila envelope dropped to the ground. Evidently the postman had folded the newspaper around it before slipping them into the box. Cooper picked up the envelope and froze at the return address in the upper left corner that in bold, black type proclaimed: United States Government, Department of the Army. Heart pounding and hands shaking at what it might portend, he tore open the envelope and, as he feared, found it contained a Notice to Report. His heart sank at the sight of it. He stood in the rutted drive staring at the notice for a long moment, then trudged back up the hill to the cottage.

Grace and Colin were still at the table in the shady grove when Cooper returned. The lunch dishes had been cleared and Grace was at one end arranging a bunch of wildflowers from the garden in a vase. Colin sat at the other end, writing a letter. Shocked by Cooper's news, he lifted his pen in mid-sen-

tence and angrily crumpled the sheet of stationery in his fist.

"I thought you were too . . . too old,"
Grace said, her lips trembling as she spoke.

"Aye, I *was*," Cooper replied, trying to collect himself. "But no longer. According to
this, the age has been raised to forty-five for
technical specialists."

"When do you have to report?" Grace
asked anxiously.

"It says sixty days . . ."

"Thanks be to God the wedding's but a
month away." Grace continued arranging
the flowers in the vase as if this occupation
might restrain the flood of emotion that was
welling up inside her.

"Sixty days from the date of this notice,"
Cooper said grimly. "Which was . . . the
eighteenth of May."

"Eighteenth of May?" Grace exclaimed. She
flinched at the snip of the shears, having cut
a stem without intending to. "That's . . .
that's almost two months ago."

"Aye," Cooper replied, making the calculation. "It seems I've three days before I'm
to report."

Grace sighed with confusion and set the
shears aside. "How could that be?"

Cooper showed her the envelope and pointed to the address. "The notice was sent to the rooming house, lass. That's where I was living when I registered, and that's the address I put on the forms. Since I'd been turned down, it never occurred to me to give them the new one. I'm afraid all the weeks spent returning and forwarding it has left me little time to report"—he pointed to a paragraph in the notice—"with my camera equipment, I might add."

Grace looked puzzled. "Your camera equipment?"

"Aye, it seems I'm in the Army Aeronautical Service, assigned to an aerial reconnaissance unit."

"Oh," Grace said, taking a moment to collect her thoughts. "What shall we do about the wedding?"

"I'm afraid it will have to be postponed," Cooper replied. "I don't see that we have any choice."

Colin, who up until now seemed to be in shock, straightened in his chair. "Not necessarily," he said sharply, getting their attention.

"What do you mean by that?" Cooper asked.

"Quite simply, there's no need to post-pone the wedding if you don't report," Colin explained, pleased with his cleverness. "The notice was posted and delivered to the wrong address. Why not just make believe you never got it?"

"I couldn't do that," Cooper stated with fi-nality. "It wouldn't be right. As much as I want to marry Grace and have a life here with her, I just couldn't."

"Why not?" Colin challenged, getting to his feet. "If you really mean that, why go running off to war if you don't have to?" He answered the question before Cooper had a chance. "Unless of course you've come down with a case of cold feet and this is a convenient excuse to avoid it."

"You know better than that," Cooper said, an edge creeping into his voice. "I regis-tered for a reason, Colin; and it hasn't changed." He slapped the newspaper on the table in front of him. The headline read: 10,000 DOUGHBOYS DEAD. "Furthermore, it's against the law not to report. And since I'm not yet naturalized, if found out, I'll not only be prosecuted, I'll be deported. Now, *you* may have a burning desire to go home to

Scotland, Colin, but *I* don't. My home is here, now."

"Yes, it's no secret I want to go home," Colin said in an embittered voice. "After all the time I've spent looking after Grace, I've every right to resume my life."

"Now we're getting to work on the crust of the bread, Colin, aren't we?" Cooper said, assembling the pieces in his mind. "You see, Grace, postponing the wedding isn't Colin's problem. No, his problem is me going off to war. Because, if I do, married or no, *he's* duty bound to stay here with you."

"Oh dear, you're right," Grace said, shifting her eyes to Colin. "You couldn't leave me here alone and go home, could you?"

"You know very well I couldn't, Grace," Colin replied, stung by the irony and Cooper's insight.

"Aye," Cooper said, his eyes narrowing with suspicion. "And I've a feeling his plans to do so are, perhaps, further along than we thought."

"Further along?" Grace prompted, looking puzzled.

"I'd bet a dollar to a dime that he finally has enough saved for a steamer ticket,"

Cooper replied with a wiley grin. "Haven't you, Colin?"

"Finally," Colin replied evenly. "Enough for one. And, yes, I've been planning to purchase it sometime after the wedding."

"Maybe it's time to think of someone other than yourself, Colin," Grace said, bristling with indignation. "Do you think I want Dylan to go off to war? Lord knows I don't know how I'll sleep nights when he's gone . . . worrying if I'll ever see him again . . . if he's been hurt or . . . or God forbid, killed. I'm going to be beside myself every minute of every day, and all you can worry about is going home? How can you be so selfish?"

Colin swallowed hard, stung by her words, and took a moment to collect himself. "Has it ever occurred to you, Grace, that I might have a *reason* for going home? A *special* reason much the same as the one *you* have for deciding not to?"

Grace flinched at the implication and exchanged a look with Cooper. "What special reason, Colin?"

"It's quite simple," Colin replied. "You see, when I accepted responsibility for your well-being, I gave up something—" He paused, and correcting himself, said, "some*one*.

Yes, Grace, I left someone behind who I care for just as deeply as you care for Cooper."

Grace's eyes welled, sending tears streaming down her cheeks. "Oh, Colin, I'd no idea," she sighed, overcome with empathy. "The letters you write, they're . . . they're not all to the family are they?"

"Not all of them, no," Colin replied, feeling vindicated. He opened his fist and glanced to the crumpled letter in his palm. "I can't very well post one to her that says I'll soon be home, now, can I?"

"No, I suppose not," Grace replied through her tears. "Why didn't you say something?"

"Because as you can see, talking about it only makes it more painful," Colin replied, biting his lip as the anger welled up inside him. "What good would it have done?! Would it have changed anything?!" he challenged, raising his voice. "No, of course not! Call me selfish, if you must; but it's not fair that I'm forced to remain here while *he's* off satisfying his sense of adventure!"

Cooper's eyes flared at the insult. "Sense of adventure?!" he echoed, his burr thickening with anger.

"What is it then? Love for the homeland you've forsaken?!" Colin prompted with a sarcastic sneer. "Then again, patriotism *is* the the last refuge of a scoundrel, isn't it?!"

Struck by a surge of adrenaline, Cooper lunged across the table, grabbing a fistful of Colin's shirt. Grace recoiled in horror with a frightened yelp. The two men's reddened faces were inches apart. "I'm going because I would have to live with myself, afterwards, if I didn't!" Cooper shouted, spattering Colin with spittle. "And so would Grace!"

Colin tried to pull free, then took a wild swing at Cooper who slipped the punch and tightened his grasp, tearing Colin's shirt. The rip of fabric fueled Colin's anger and sent him diving across the table at Cooper. His momentum knocked over the vase of flowers and sent the two men tumbling to the ground. They went rolling across the grass between the trees, pummeling each other and grappling for the advantage.

Cooper came out on top, pinning Colin's arms with his knees. "And while I'm at it!" Cooper went on, seething as Colin struggled beneath him to get free. "I'll give you another reason! A man who had half his leg blown off told me one picture would have saved it! And the lives of sixty-three of his men! Sixty-three, Colin! If I might save even one, how could I not report?!" He took hold of Colin's collar and, shaking him with anger, shouted, "How?! How?! How?!"

"Dylan! Dylan, stop it! Stop! What are you doing?!" Grace shouted, bear-hugging him from behind in an effort to pull him off Colin. To her dismay her actions had the unintended consequence of allowing Colin to free his arms and begin throwing punches at Cooper. "Stop! Stop it! Both of you! You're acting like children!"

The two men flailed at each other as if deaf to her pleas, but Cooper finally responded and rolled off Colin onto the ground. Slowly, the two men got to their feet and stood a distance apart gasping for breath and glaring at each other. Cooper tugged his pipe from a shirt pocket and jammed it hard into the corner of his mouth, venting his anger on the stem.

While the two men settled and brushed off their clothes, Grace quickly gathered the scattered flowers, put them in the vase, and set it down hard on the table like a judge rapping a gavel to restore order. "Now—

both of you—sit down like gentlemen," she commanded in crisp phrases. "I'll have no more of this adolescent behavior." Though shaken by what she had witnessed, Grace took a seat at one end of the table and, like a stern headmistress about to dispense punishment, waited until Colin and Cooper, in slow and grudging compliance with her order, had taken seats on opposite sides of it. "Colin, you were insulting and rude," Grace said in a condemning tone. "To be charitable, I can only conclude your anger poorly affected your judgement."

Colin's lips tightened into a thin line. "Yes," he said, flushed with embarrassment. "It seems to have bested me."

Grace shifted her glare to Cooper who was still chewing on his pipe stem. "And *you*— you responded to an insult with fisticuffs. You're clearly guilty of the same offense, only more so."

"Aye, my anger seems to have bested me as well," Cooper said, equally contrite.

"Good," Grace said as if she had just gotten toddlers to agree to share a toy. "I'll not have the two men in my life fighting like sworn enemies. Doubly so under the circumstances. You both have many good

qualities and I thought you'd come to appreciate them . . ." She emitted an exasperated sigh. ". . . or so it seemed."

Colin nodded in agreement and glanced
at Cooper. "If I'm to be honest with myself,
I must admit I find your strength of con-
science and sense of duty more than admirable. But—"

"Aye," Cooper interupted. "I'm able to say
the same."

"But it's not fair," Colin resumed, "that I'm
paying the price for you to be true to them."

"Aye, I can't argue with that," Cooper said
with evident sincerity. "It's *not* fair—to you,
or to any of us for that matter. And I'm truly
sorry for whatever pain it may cause; but it's
not my doing, Colin. Blame the United
States Army. Blame the Kaiser. Blame the
chaps who killed the Archduke or sank the
Lusitania, if it will make you feel better. But,
truth be told, I don't see that I've a choice
but to report. "

Colin's eyes softened with understanding.
He cocked his head in thought, then
glanced over at Grace. "What I'm about to
say will have no affect whatsoever on my
situation, Grace; but, in my heart, I still feel

strongly that you should be husband and wife before Cooper leaves."

"How?" Grace protested. "There isn't enough time."

"Not for the wedding you've planned, but there's plenty of time for a handfast ceremony," Colin said, referring to an ancient Scottish ritual that was binding on any couple who locked hands and pledged their troth, no witnesses or minister necessary.

"No," Grace said without the slightest hesitation. "It's what's in your heart that matters, not a 'secret handshake' and some hastily spoken words. Dylan and I are already bound to each other, Colin—bound for life in our hearts and souls, of that I've no doubt."

"Aye, that we are," Cooper said, his tone implying more would follow. "But while I'm off doing *my* duty, Grace, Colin will be here doing *his*, won't he?"

Grace nodded and raised her brows curiously.

"Which means," Cooper went on, "I'll have the peace of mind that comes from knowing he's looking after you and caring for the cottage. In all fairness, shouldn't he have the peace of mind that comes from knowing—with the absolute certainty that an exchange of vows would provide—that one day, he'll be free of the responsibility he has so earnestly shouldered?"

Colin stared at Cooper for a long moment, then emitted a relieved sigh and nodded. "Well-said, Cooper. Your forthrightness is much appreciated."

Grace's face was filled with remorse. "*Very* much appreciated," she whispered, wiping tears from her eyes that came to life with a thought. "Tomorrow is Sunday, isn't it? Well, instead of settling for a handfast, why don't we attend the morning service and then ask Pastor Martin to marry us?!"

Cooper leaned back in his chair, lighting his pipe as he considered it. "Why not?"

"Yes," Colin chimed in. "And there's no reason why you can't have the wedding ceremony and celebration you've been planning as soon as Cooper comes back."

The next day, after the Sunday service, they approached Pastor Martin who immediately agreed to their request. "It won't be the first nuptial I've performed ahead of schedule because of the war," the youthful minister replied.

During the short and simple ceremony

that followed, Colin gave the bride away; then he and the pastor's wife served as witnesses while Grace and Dylan exchanged vows and Pastor Martin pronounced them husband and wife to have and to hold from this day forward until death do they part.

After the ceremony, the three of them headed off to the Lobster Trap, a rustic, dockside tavern in the heart of Newbury Harbor, where they celebrated quietly with the catch of the day and tankards of ale. That afternoon, Colin took the train back to Boston, leaving Grace and Cooper to honeymoon in the cottage. They had until the next morning to be together, at which time they would both return to Boston, Cooper to the induction center, Grace to the gallery. After dropping Colin at the station, they drove to the seashore and spent the remainder of the afternoon walking the sandy beaches and frolicking in the shallow surf, then as the sun dropped behind the trees, they returned to the cottage.

And that evening—on their wedding night, the night before Cooper left for duty—as the intoxicating aroma of the sea permeated the air, and moonlight streamed through the lace curtains of their bedroom windows, they became lovers. It was the tender and considerate lovemaking of people who cared deeply for each other. Once their soaring passion had been unleashed, their intimate caresses served as further testimony to the lifelong commitment they had made in their hearts and in the presence of God; and crested in satiating fulfillment as the joys of their physical union became a moving spiritual one as well.

The next morning, Cooper and Grace loaded his valise and a small trunk that contained his camera gear into the pickup truck, and drove back to Boston in saddened silence. He parked on the street in front of the gallery and gave her the keys so she and Colin could have use of his truck while he was gone.

"The keys to my heart, Mrs. Cooper," he said, trying to sound lighthearted though he was emotionally overwhelmed by the thought of leaving her.

Grace sighed, her eyes brimming with tears, "I can't believe that I won't . . . won't be seeing . . ." She couldn't finish it and buried her head in the curve of his neck, then looked up into his eyes and kissed him. "I'll wait a lifetime for you, Dylan."

"And I for you, Grace," Cooper said, his eyes glistening with emotion.

"I love you so much," Grace said, tears rolling down her cheeks. "Please take good care of yourself and—" She was interrupted by the clanging bell of an approaching streetcar. "Go. Go now. Please, you must."

Cooper hesitated, then swiftly pulled the valise and trunk from the back of the pickup while Grace flagged the trolley. After loading them aboard, he stood in the doorway, blowing her kisses as it pulled away. His antics brought a smile to Grace's face, but she was paralyzed with sadness as the trolley followed the curve of the tracks onto Beacon Street. She remained there long after it was out of sight, wondering if she'd ever see him again.

Chapter Twenty-Two

The trolley took Cooper to the Federal Building on Congress Street. He hauled his suitcase and trunk into the Induction Center and spent the day being processed. That evening, he and dozens of the other inductees were trucked a short distance to Boston's South Station and put aboard a troop train. Twenty hours later, after stops in New York and Philadelphia to pick up more inductees, it arrived in Harrisburg, Pennsylvania, where a convoy of trucks transported them to Carlisle Military Barracks to undergo basic training.

During the twelve weeks Cooper spent there, he wrote to Grace at every opportunity, regaling her with humorous stories of how, as the "old man" of his unit, he'd been made to dig trenches, crawl through mud, and taught to field strip and fire a rifle—all the while existing on food that not even a haggis-fated hog would consider edible. Fortunately, mail was delivered to stateside military bases regularly, and it was Grace's letters and pictures of her that he'd brought with him that got him through the daily grind. On a more curious note, he wrote that he had never laid eyes on a combat aircraft and had received no instruction on taking reconnaissance pictures while flying in one.

When basic training ended, Cooper was sporting corporal's stripes on his sleeve and a Signal Corps patch on his shoulder due to his specialist status. He shipped out of Philadelphia Harbor on a troopship with thousands of other doughboys. The weather in the North Atlantic was as miserable as the conditions aboard the overcrowded vessel. Cooper wrote to Grace, joking that the military's unappetizing food was, at long last, of no consequence, because nearly everyone aboard was seasick, and the mere smell of it sent them dashing to the railing. Indeed, the steerage-class accomodations of his immigrant voyage to America seemed like a posh, first-class cruise in comparison.

After weeks at sea, Cooper disembarked in LeHavre, France, gaunt, pale, and in need of rest and relaxation. Instead, he found himself on yet another troop train. It chugged noisily through the French countryside until it reached an air base near Châtillon-sur-Seine, sixty miles southeast of Paris where Cooper was assigned to the Army Aeronautical Service barracks. Hungry and exhausted, he dragged his valise and trunk of camera gear to his bunk, and was about to fall face down on the bare mattress when a voice called out, "Hey there, you must be Corporal Cooper."

Cooper turned to see three uniformed men—jodphurs, leggings, wool blouses, and corporal's stripes, like his own—approaching. "Aye, that I am," he replied wearily.

"Welcome to the First Aerial Reconnaissance Squadron," Kenyon said, extending a hand.

"The first and *only*," Arkoff joked.

"You're just in time for the briefing," Wallace said. "Follow us."

En route, Cooper learned that, like him, they were all newly assigned to the Aerial Reconnaissance Squadron. Kenyon was an adventure-seeking photojournalist; Wallace did weddings and bar mitzvahs; and Arkoff had worked at a movie studio taking publicity shots of silent film stars. They entered a hangar where the four pilots with whom they'd be flying, and Colonel Jenkins, the Squadron Commander, had assembled. Jenkins paired them off, then outlined the general scope of their mission. "There'll be a two week training period," he concluded. "After which you'll be upgraded to mission status."

"Training?" Kenyon echoed. "Sir, we're not puppies who need to be housebroke. I signed up to go flying and shoot Huns with my camera. My editor is waiting with baited breath for—"

"At ease, Corporal," Jenkins interrupted smartly. "It's not your editor's life that's going to be on the line up there, it's yours and your pilot's. Therefore, you'll train in the air with him first. Teamwork is everything in this business. That's why, despite the regulations that prohibit officers and enlisted men from sharing living quarters, I ordered that you all be billeted in the same barracks. *Teamwork*."

Cooper was teamed with Captain Tyler Mottram, a Georgia farmboy who flew crop dusters in civilian life. A welcome departure from the military's habit of turning pilots into truck drivers and clerks into pilots, Cooper thought.

Captain Mottram took Cooper to a maintenance bay where two mechanics were working on his biplane. One was patching bullet holes in its wings. The other was removing its wooden airscrew, which had been splintered by gunfire. The Breuget-Bristol Type 14-A2 had been designed by the French, manufactured by the British, and flown and serviced by Americans. Its top speed exceeded 125 mph. It carried forty gallons of fuel, which could keep it aloft for approximately two and one half hours.

"For reasons y'all will soon come to know," Mottram said, "we call this aeroplane the Tin Whistle."

"Aye," Cooper grunted, thinking the rickety craft resembled the models children made from kits. Painted canvas, glued and nailed to a painfully thin aluminum airframe, formed its fuselage and sheathed its wings. The upper wing was connected to the lower with struts braced by what looked like bailing wire. The aircraft had two cockpits—pilot up front and gunner behind where the machine gun was mounted. "With all due respect, sir, am I expected to get in there with my camera?"

"Y'all catch on right quick, Cooper," Mottram drawled with a broad grin, pronouncing it Coopah.

"Aye, sir, but who's goin' to catch the camera?" Cooper retorted, matching Mottram's grin. "Just keeping hold of it, let alone while trying to focus or change film holders, would confound a four-armed acrobat."

"Yep, y'all might have a dickens of a time of it, Corporal," Mottram conceded. "When it comes to combat, it seems we're always flying upside down."

Cooper's brows were arched. "Aye, I'm afraid it'll be over the side before I get to fire the shutter."

"Well, long as y'all don't go over with it," Mottram joked with a cackle. "'Cause if you do, there won't be anyone left to operate the machine gun."

Cooper's jaw slackened.

"It's easier than fallin' out of your bunk at reville," Mottram said, seeing his reaction. "Ya'll just aim and fire. The bullets do the rest. The trick is to avoid shooting me or the aircraft."

As soon as his Tin Whistle was airworthy, Mottram took Cooper flying—without his camera—to familiarize him with its weapons systems and the sensations of flight and to get used to the piercing whistle it emitted in a dive, hence its nickname. He gradually increased the severity of the maneuvers and decreased their interval until Cooper could function despite the feeling that his weight had suddenly doubled, pinning him to his seat and pressing his goggles tight against his face; and could endure the violent repetitions of snaps, rolls and dives that were critical to combat flying without becoming light-headed or sick to his stomach.

During the training period, Cooper spent his spare time thinking up ways to secure the camera in the air. Observing that the military police patrolled the air base on horseback, he got an idea and headed over to the barn where the horses were billetted and the saddlery was located. Sergeant Halstead, the master saddlemaker, sparked to Cooper's challenge. By the end of the training period, they had fashioned a harness of straps and buckles that fit over Cooper's shoulders and around his torso, and attached to the camera with snap latches. The harness would support its weight, prevent it from falling over the side, and keep his hands free to operate it.

"That's a work of genius, Dylan," Wallace said when Cooper returned to the barracks with the harness. "Boy oh boy, imagine what you could do with one of these at a wedding!" Kenyon and Arkoff were equally impressed and the three of them wasted no time heading for the saddlery.

Cooper wrote to Grace telling her how much his colleagues admired his resourcefulness and how much he enjoyed their camraderie. He went on about the thrill of flying, and being tutored by Captain Mottram; though truth be told, he'd much prefer to be at home with her working on the cottage and taking pictures of whatever happened to catch his eye. He concluded by reassuring her he was safe, and that despite being away for over four months, he had yet to see any combat. He didn't mention that the Air Mission Manifest had just been posted or that the Mottram-Cooper team was on it. Nor that they'd be taking aerial reconnaissance photographs of the rail yards at Metz, a highly fortified enemy distribution depot in German territory about thirty miles beyond the Franco-Prussian border.

The first spark of morning light was burning on the horizon when the ground crew pulled the chocks from the biplane's tires. Captain Mottram responded with a thumbs up, then walled the throttle and the Breguet-Bristol began rolling down the runway, gathering speed. He eased back on the joystick and the plane rose from the tarmac and climbed into the morning haze. Cooper checked his camera gear, then swiveled about in his cockpit, scanning the horizon for enemy aircraft as the Captain put the Tin Whistle into a sweeping turn and set a course for Germany.

Chapter Twenty-Three

Aerial reconnaissance missions were scheduled in early morning or late afternoon because the low angle of the sun created brilliant highlights and long, dark shadows. The contrast made troops, tanks, artillery and ground fortifications stand out against the terrain, producing sharply defined and highly informative photographs. The altitude from which they were taken was determind by the cloud cover and haze over the target, and the need to avoid detection by enemy spotters who would launch Fokker interceptors, jeopardizing the mission, not to mention the lives of the pilot and photographer. This need for stealth dictated a low altitude approach followed by a corkscrew climb over the target during which photographs would be taken from various altitudes and angles.

Captain Mottram had the biplane over

Metz and on approach to target in just over forty minutes. In the distance, rails of polished steel reflected the fiery sunlight, sharply defining the sinuous pattern of the rail yards. Cooper was thinking each rail looked like it had just emerged from a blast furnace when Mottram dipped a wing, putting the plane over on its side. His camera secured by its harness, Cooper set it on the rim of his cockpit, centered the rail yards in the frame, fine-tuned the focus, inserted the film holder, pulled the slide and fired the shutter, signaling Mottram with a slap on his flying helmet when it was done.

While Mottram put the aircraft into a sweeping climb, Cooper went through the steps again: frame, focus, holder, slide, shutter. He had removed the film holder and was readying another when a German Fokker dove out of the sun.

Machine-gun bullets were whizzing around Cooper and Mottram like a swarm of attacking bees, punching holes in the aircraft's canvas fuselage and wings, and pinging loudly off the aluminum airframe. Mottram used a snap roll to put the plane into a dive, a maneuver that, if not for its harness, would have thrown the camera from the plane; and, if not for his seat belt, tossed Cooper after it. Instinctively, he set the camera in his lap, whirled in his seat, grasped the machine gun and began firing at the pursuing Fokker.

Cooper found the pulse-pounding dogfight exciting and terrifying at the same time. To Captain Mottram's delight, Cooper's relentless return fire forced the German pilot to disengage. The Fokker peeled off toward the horizon, a long trail of smoke spiraling from its engine housing.

In the following months, Cooper went on many such missions. Some were without incident; others were as hair-raising as the first; and a few were even more so. One afternoon he was sitting in his bunk writing a letter to Grace when Colonel Jenkins entered the barracks. "Gather round, gentlemen," he said in a voice that belied his casual demeanor. "One of our code-breakers has decrypted a top secret German radio signal, alerting us to a major offensive at Reims."

"Sounds like the tide's turning in our direction, sir," Arkoff said, effusively.

"Maybe," Jenkins grunted. "But Operations thinks it might be a trick. A way to get us to redeploy our troops on the Western Front, exposing the real target to attack. We need to know if German troops are massing in the areas around Reims, or not. Thousands of lives are at stake. Now, I'm not going to sugarcoat it. This is a dangerous mission. Some people are calling it a suicide mission. So, we've decided to ask for volunteers. I need one pilot and one—"

Captain Mottram stepped forward before he could finish. "I'm your man, Colonel."

"Very well, Captain. We have a pilot. Now we—"

Cooper raised his hand and was about to verbally volunteer as the photographer.

"I'll fly with him," Kenyon blurted, beating Cooper to it.

"Hold on there," Cooper said, his burr thickening. "If Captain Mottram's the pilot, then *I'm* the photographer. We're a team, sir, and a fine one at that. I see no reason to be changing, now."

"Captain?" Jenkins prompted turning to Mottram.

"Kenyon is a fine man, suh," Mottram replied in his Georgia drawl. "But Coopah's right. The nature of the mission makes teamwork paramount; and thanks to his performance under fire, I'm still alive to say it."

"Then Mottram-Cooper it is," Colonel Jenkins said without hesitation. "Good luck, gentlemen. Briefing's at nineteen hundred. Takeoff at zero six hundred tomorrow."

Jenkins turned on heel and strode off. He had barely left the barracks when a flash of lightning followed by rolling claps of thunder rattled the windows, heralding the onset of a storm. Within minutes, the air base was being lashed by forty mile an hour winds and blinding sheets of rain.

That's when it dawned on Cooper and the others that Wallace and his pilot, who had taken off several hours earlier on one of the late afternoon missions, hadn't returned. It was more than possible that the pilot had put his aircraft down safely on a roadway or in a farmer's field to wait out the storm. But their hopes were dashed when another pilot, who had managed to make it back despite the weather, reported seeing Wallace's aircraft go down in a flaming crash.

The violent weather grounded every aircraft on the base, forcing the mission to be postponed. For weeks, floodwaters raged throughout France, drowning soldiers in their trenches on both sides of no-man's-land. The incessant rain, the ankle-deep mud, and the death of his colleague took their toll on Cooper's spirit. Lonely and depressed, he was laying in his bunk, staring at a picture of Grace when someone shouted, "Mail call!"

A crush of men gathered around the squadron clerk in anxious silence. He opened a sack of envelopes and packages, and began calling out names. He had gone through more than a dozen before he shouted, "Cooper!" and handed him an envelope.

Unlike stateside military mail, delivery in war-torn Europe was unreliable and erratic. Many letters were lost. Those that weren't often took months to get there as the Newbury postmark on Cooper's confirmed; but he didn't need to see it or the return address to know who had sent it, because the penmanship was clearly Grace's; and his spirits soared as he hurried back to his bunk and tore it open.

"My goodness, Coopah," Mottram said. "Do I detect the scent of a woman permeating these barracks?"

"Smell's like the perfume of a ballet

dancer that I . . . ah . . . that I took some pictures of, once," Arkoff teased.

Cooper forced a smile and kept reading in silence.

Mottram noticed his face had paled and the letter was shaking in his hands. "Coopah, y'all look like you've just seen your pappy's ghost."

Cooper failed to respond, despite the provocation, and stared at Grace's letter, appearing to be in shock.

"Five'll get you ten it's a Dear John," Kenyon said.

"Maybe it's a love poem," Mottram ventured with a lascivious cackle. "I promised y'all my heart to the core, but now that y'all gone off to war, I've become a little ol' whore."

The men erupted with raucous laughter.

Though clearly shaken by whatever news the letter contained, Cooper couldn't help but laugh with them. ". . . And soon a baby will be crawling on the floor!" he rhymed, good-naturedly, finishing the poem.

Suddenly, they sensed Cooper was doing more than partaking in the bawdy barracks banter, and questioned him with looks. "Coopah?" Mottram prompted, knowingly.

"Yes, yes, she's pregnant!" Cooper exclaimed in reply. "Grace is pregnant. I'm going to be a daddy!"

"Assuming you *are* the daddy," Kenyon joked with a sarcastic chuckle. "Congratulations, Dylan! Now all you need to do is get home alive."

Cooper nodded resolutely. "Aye, that I do."

"There's still the matter of that little suicide mission I volunteered us for," Mottram prompted, catching Kenyon's eye.

"I'll take your place, Cooper," Kenyon offered, picking up on Mottram's signal. "I volunteered before you did, anyway. Remember?"

"Aye," Cooper said, genuinely touched by the gesture. "I don't know what to say."

"Say yes, you Scottish fool," Arkoff prompted.

"I'm tempted," Cooper conceded. "But I'm afraid, it's my mission. I'm going on it. And there's no discussing it. Teamwork, Captain, remember?"

The mission was rescheduled as soon as the skies over the Western Front had cleared. That night, Mottram and Cooper, Kenyon and Arkoff and their pilots, along with some members of the ground crew, and Halstead, the saddlemaker, were in a local cafe toasting Cooper's upcoming fatherhood with tankards of ale. At one point, they all bunched together with jaunty smiles, their tankards raised, while someone took a picture.

"To the men of the First, and only, Aerial Recon Squadron!" Arkoff shouted as the shutter fired.

Unseen by Cooper amidst the jocularity, a look passed between Mottram and Kenyon suggesting they were up to something. "Another round!" Mottram exclaimed, making certain Cooper's tankard had been refilled. Over the next several hours, Mottram and Kenyon alternated as refillers of Cooper's tankard more times than they dared count. "Takeoff is at zero six hundred, Coopah," Mottram finally announced. "I'm goin' to get me some sack time. Y'all better do the same."

Early the next morning, Cooper awoke with a start and a nasty headache. It took him a few moments to realize that the barracks were strangely silent at a time when he expected everyone involved in the early morning mission to be rising. That's when he realized Mottram's bunk was empty and neatly made. So was Kenyon's. As were those of the ground crew. Cooper donned his flight gear, grabbed his camera and harness, and dashed to the flight line. He arrived just as Mottram's Tin Whistle was lifting off the runway. Kenyon, nestled in the rear cockpit, spotted Cooper and snapped off a jaunty salute. Cooper was still groggy from his rude awakening and stood on the tarmac watching as the plane vanished into the haze.

"Looks like you overslept, Corporal," a member of the ground crew prompted.

"Overslept?" Cooper protested. "It's zero five ten. The Captain said takeoff was at zero six hundred."

"*Five* hundred, Corporal," the crewman corrected, with a knowing smile. "Amazing isn't it? How even an officer can make a mistake, every now and then."

"This one was made accidentally on purpose, wasn't it?" Cooper prompted.

The crewman nodded. "Way I heard it, they want to make sure that baby of yours gets to know his daddy."

Cooper nodded in humble appreciation, then checked the clipboard where the Air

Mission Manifest was posted. "Looks like my name's still on the AMM."

"Well, the SC doesn't like last minute changes to mission crews," he explained, referring to the Squadron Commander. "Too much paperwork, I guess. So Captain Mottram decided we'd be smart to just leave it."

Barring complications, a gas tank with two and one half hours of fuel made it easy to calculate the maximum time a flight, to target and back, could take. Cooper decided to remain on the flight line until Mottram and Kenyon returned. At which time he would generously applaud their bravery and selfless friendship, then angrily denounce their duplicitous conspiracy. They should have been back by mid-morning at the latest—but they weren't. At noon, Cooper had every reason to fear the worst. As dusk fell, it was clear they wouldn't ever be returning.

Cooper headed back to the barracks and fell into his bunk distraught at the tragic turn of events and reflecting on the life he'd had in Boston with Grace and the new beginning they'd made in Newbury. Now, he felt strangely detached, as if he'd fallen asleep in a place of peace, love and sanity, only to awaken in a hellish nightmare of whistling aircraft, blazing machine guns and sense-less, flaming death—a death that, if not for this bizarre twist, would have been his own. He turned to thoughts of Grace and of the upcoming birth of their child to raise his spirits and buttress his belief that he would return home safely.

Several weeks later, Cooper had been paired with a new pilot and was awaiting his next mission assignment when Germany sued for peace and word spread that the war to end all wars was, at last, over.

Chapter Twenty-Four

The armistice was signed on November 11, 1918.

The American Expeditionary Force had done its job. Many military units were swiftly decommissioned and countless thousands of doughboys were being discharged and sent home.

Cooper was excited by the thought of celebrating Christmas with Grace in Newbury and at being with her for the birth of their baby. In mid-November he got a letter in which Grace joked that her tummy was starting to resemble a keg of ale—his *favorite* ale of course—and that the doctor had calculated the blessed event would be sometime in March.

The letter had taken well over a month to reach him and Cooper was lying in his bunk, imagining what she must look like now, when Colonel Jenkins called a meeting of the squadron. The men assumed he would be issuing their discharge orders. Instead he informed them that they had an important role to play in the immediate postwar period; and to Cooper's dismay, he and the rest of his squadron were soon back in the air, flying compliance verification missions. Their assignment was to provide photographic evidence that German troops were withdrawing from French territory and returning to their homeland. Though the threat of being shot down by enemy aircraft had been removed, the winter weather and the ever-present danger of flight made every mission a risky one.

There were no missions scheduled for Christmas day, and Cooper would have given anything to have been celebrating it with Grace in the snow-blanketed cottage in Newbury. Instead, he spent it with the members of his squadron in their barracks on the air base in Châtillon-sur-Seine, bemoaning their miserable luck, and the even more upsetting fact that there had been no Christmas mail call.

As the squadron clerk, in danger of being lashed to a spinning airscrew in retaliation, explained: the postwar decommissioning of units in every branch of the military and the discharging and mustering out of personnel had made logistics into a disorganized nightmare. As a result, mail delivery had become even more unreliable, and often non-existent. Cooper had been anxiously awaiting a Christmas letter from Grace. Now he realized he might not be getting any of her letters at all, nor might she be getting any of his.

Cooper was finally discharged in early March. He had been away almost ten months; and at about the time Grace was due to have the baby, he was on a troopship somewhere in the stormy North Atlantic. The vessel, taking him and thousands of other doughboys home, berthed temporarily in St. John's, New Foundland, to take on fuel and supplies. While there, he sent a telegram to Grace with the date of its arrival in Boston Harbor.

He had every reason to expect Grace and his newborn child would be there when it docked. To his disappointment they weren't among the waving throngs when he came down the gangplank. He took the train to Newbury, but they weren't at the station when he got off the train, either. So, he took a taxi to the cottage, only to find it was empty. There was no sign of Grace or of a cooing baby. Neither was there a cradle, diapers, nor any other evidence of a newborn; and little evidence of Grace being in residence either. Furthermore, his pickup truck was nowhere to be seen.

Cooper was baffled and beside himself until he heard the sound of a vehicle coming up the dirt road toward the cottage. He ran to the door, his heart thumping joyously and swung it open just as his truck rolled to a stop. Colin was its only passenger. He got out with a bag of groceries, then froze at the sight of Cooper standing in the doorway and stared at him for a long moment. He saw the question in Cooper's eyes and answered it before he could ask. "Grace is gone, I'm afraid."

Cooper looked puzzled. "What do you mean gone?"

Colin winced. "Gone home to Scotland."

"To Scotland? Why?" Cooper wondered, looking as if confronted by puzzle pieces that didn't fit; then, despite its seemingly thin logic, he grasped at the only reason he could imagine that made any sense, and concluded, "Because she wanted the family

to see the baby. Of course, that's it, isn't it?"
He could tell from Colin's reaction that there
was more to it, and went back inside the
cottage. The bottles of liquor were still on
the sideboard where they were when he'd
left. He poured himself a shot of brandy and
was about to pour another for Colin, who
had followed him inside, when he was
struck by a disturbing thought, and set the
bottle down. "Why didn't you go with her,
Colin? A woman traveling alone with a baby.
It was your job to protect her, wasn't it?"

Colin set the grocery bag on the table and
nodded emphatically. "Indeed, and God
knows I wanted to; but as you recall we had
only enough saved for one ticket, and try as
we might, we weren't able to add to it once
you'd gone."

"You mean, the money you were planning
to use for *your* ticket," Cooper said, admir-
ingly, recalling how much returning to Scotland meant to Colin.

Colin nodded humbly, then opened a desk
drawer and removed a slip of pale yellow paper. It was a telegram. "I gave Grace the
money after this came," he went on, handing it to Cooper.

It was from the Department of the Army,

dated December 2, 1918, and read: We regret to inform you that Corporal Dylan Cooper was killed in action on October 29, 1918. He served his country with honor and bravery. The President wishes to extend his heartfelt sympathy and condolences for your loss.

"Oh, dear Lord," Cooper gasped, reflecting on the Air Mission Manifest that hadn't been revised. "But I wrote to Grace throughout the winter. The post was troublesome; but she didn't get *any* of my letters?"

Colin shook his head no. "She left a week before Christmas. A few arrived well after the New Year. You can imagine my surprise when I saw the dates on the postmarks. I got the cable you sent from New Foundland but thought it best we talk about this here."

Cooper nodded solemnly and folded the telegram in half. "Yes, of course, reading this must've been so devastating for Grace. Even with you here, it's easy to understand why she felt it best to go back home to have the baby."

Colin sighed and took a deep breath. "Yes, it was a terribly crushing blow; but it was made all the more devastating because it came..." Colin swallowed hard and bit a lip to hold back tears. "I'm sorry, I've been trying to find a way to say this, Cooper. It came a few weeks after she . . . after she *lost* the baby."

The color drained from Cooper's face. He felt hollow, as if he'd been gutted by the fusillades of machine-gun fire he had somehow escaped. Stunned to silence, he turned to the window, staring blankly at the distant sea, a watershed of tears running down his cheeks.

"It was an all too early labor," Colin went on softly. "The doctor did everything possible. The baby lived for just a few hours . . ."

"Oh dear, Grace . . ." Cooper groaned in a mournful sigh.

"She sent you a letter, but from what you said about the post . . ."

Cooper nodded imperceptibly. It seemed as if an eternity had passed by the time he muttered, "It was months behind at best."

Colin put a comforting hand on his shoulder. "Rest assured your tiny son is with the Lord in Heaven," he said, trying in vain to brighten the gloom.

"And Grace?" Cooper whispered, his voice breaking with emotion.

Colin shook his head sadly. "She was hoping and praying you'd come home. As devastated as she was, she was certain that once you were here with her, she'd somehow find the strength to cope with the loss. But when the telegram from the Army came . . . Well, it was just more than she could bear. She became deeply depressed, wouldn't touch her food, or go into town to do her marketing. She would just sit by the window staring out at the sea for hours and hours. The doctor thought perhaps if she went home . . ." Colin let it trail off and splayed his hands in a helpless gesture.

Cooper fought to keep his emotions under control and took a few moments to recover from the devastating news; then he drained the glass of brandy, and met Colin's gaze with eyes that were filled with tears and remorse. "You're a good brother, Colin, and a fine man; and for those times that I judged you harshly or spoke of you uncharitably I sincerely apologize." He shook his head with dismay at this, the *most* tragic war casualty of all. "If I'd taken your advice, if I'd been here as you wanted, none of this would've happened."

Colin's lips tightened into a thin line. "The

good Lord works in mysterious ways," he offered, trying to soften Cooper's pain.

"The *good* Lord?" Cooper prompted with a weary sigh. "I'm afraid this is one of His mysteries I can neither fathom, nor accept."

There was no doubt in Cooper's mind what he would do next. Grace was his wife, and he was more in love with her now than he had ever been, if that were possible. They could still spend the rest of their lives together, raise a family, and live happily ever after, he thought. Though he hadn't been able to be there for her then, he could be there for her now, and vowed to do so. Indeed, he had often said he would wait a lifetime for her and, now, he promised himself he would spend a lifetime searching for her if need be.

He sent a telegram to Grace at her parents address to let her know that contrary to what she'd been told, he had survived the war, and would soon be with her. Then, he withdrew all the funds that remained in their account, added his mustering out pay from the Army, and bought two steamer tickets to Scotland. He gave one to Colin, kept the other for himself, and set off to find her.